"We'll get through this..."

"Is this another one of your famous promises?"

Liam didn't answer and instead looked at Paige's right arm, trussed up in a sling. "This is going to be a little tricky."

"You ought to get out of here. Wait for the police, the bomb squad. No sense in both of us..." She didn't finish. She didn't have to.

The grim line of Liam's lips told her what he thought of her suggestion.

"You think I'd leave you?" Outrage rimmed every syllable.

No. She didn't. Afraid to say anything more, she shook her head. At the same time, she bit down on her lip. Hard. The pain gave her something to focus on rather than the fear that crawled up her spine to settle at the base of her neck.

Buck up, girl. You've faced down terrorists, gunrunners and smugglers. What's one itty-bitty bomb?

"On the count of three, be ready."

"For what?"

"This." With that, he grabbed her good arm and yanked her from the seat before she knew what was happening.

Jane M. Choate dreamed of writing from the time she was a small child when she entertained friends with outlandish stories complete with happily-ever-after endings. Writing for Love Inspired Suspense is a dream come true. Jane is the proud mother of five children, grandmother to ten grandchildren and staff to one cat who believes she is of royal descent.

Books by Jane M. Choate

Love Inspired Suspense

Keeping Watch
The Littlest Witness
Shattered Secrets
High-Risk Investigation
Inherited Threat
Stolen Child
Secrets from the Past

Visit the Author Profile page at Harlequin.com.

Secrets from the Past

Jane M. Choate

LOVE INSPIRED SUSPENSE
INSPIRATIONAL ROMANCE

LOVE INSPIRED® SUSPENSE
INSPIRATIONAL ROMANCE

Recycling programs
for this product may
not exist in your area.

ISBN-13: 978-1-335-40517-3

Secrets from the Past

Copyright © 2021 by Jane M. Choate

This edition published by arrangement with Harlequin Books S.A.

For questions and comments about the quality of this book, please contact us at CustomerService@Harlequin.com.

Love Inspired
22 Adelaide St. West, 40th Floor
Toronto, Ontario M5H 4E3, Canada
www.Harlequin.com

Printed in U.S.A.

For thou desirest not sacrifice; else would I give it: thou delightest not in burnt offering. The sacrifices of God are a broken spirit: a broken and a contrite heart, O God, thou wilt not despise.

–Psalm 51:16–17

I wrote this book during the pandemic. During that time, I marveled at the heroes and heroines who stepped forward: nurses and doctors, truck drivers and store clerks, farmers and ranchers, all of whom our nation, indeed, our world, depended upon. We did not need movie stars or sports figures or politicians; we needed the working people, those who did their jobs so that the rest of us could continue with our lives as normally as possible. This book is for them and for all of those who kept the rest of us going.

ONE

*B*am.

The crunch of metal against metal sent the Suburban careening to the far edge of the highway.

The car fishtailed as Liam McKenzie struggled to get it under control. The tricked-out truck that had picked up their tail while Liam was driving his son to preschool and was even now giving chase showed no signs of easing up. If he didn't lose it soon, it would send his car straight over the sheer cliff flanking one side of the narrow road.

"Daddy, I'm scared."

Jonah's plaintive words jammed Liam's heart in his throat. Liam was scared, too. Not for himself, but for his five-year-old son, the most important person in his life. "I'm scared, too, but it'll be okay."

"Promise?" The two syllables sent his heartbeat into overdrive.

"Promise." He hoped he could make good on his words.

Army Deltas typically ran into danger, not away from it. But ex–Delta operator Liam McKenzie was doing just that—running from danger, against every instinct, every piece of training he'd ever received. He hadn't used any of his Delta training since leaving the army and starting up his software company, but it was still very much a part of him. Maybe that was why he'd agreed to meet with a member of the US Marshal Service about possibly accepting a job. He wanted to put his highly honed skills to use. More, he wanted to make the world a better place, a safer place for his son and for everyone else.

But none of that was important. Not now. Keeping Jonah safe was all that Liam cared about. Even when every fiber of him was urging him to turn his vehicle around and give chase to the men who were doing their best to run him off the road.

The worry in Jonah's eyes lightened. "Why are those men trying to push us off the road?"

Jonah's curiosity was one of his most endearing qualities, but Liam didn't have the time or energy to answer. Not now. Not when everything in him was focused on getting his son to safety.

"I don't know." That wasn't strictly the truth, as Liam had a pretty good idea why someone wanted to run them off the road.

"If you don't know, nobody knows, because you're the smartest daddy in the whole world."

Despite the grim circumstances, Liam had to smile. Jonah's faith in him gave him the courage he needed to keep going. It was a touchstone, a reminder of all that was good in the world. He needed that now, desperately needed it, as he raced to find a way to save their lives.

A small opening in the bushes on the other side of the road presented an escape. He pressed down harder on the accelerator, swerved sharply across the road before the pickup rounded the curve and pulled into it, hoping the bushes would obscure his vehicle.

A deep breath later, the pickup sped on down the road, leaving Liam free to turn around and head in the opposite direction. It would take another half hour to get home—preschool was forgotten—but it was worth it if it spared Jonah any more distress.

Liam was ready to face what had to be faced. He'd served for eight years in hot spots all over the world and had never been as shaking-in-his-boots scared as he was now. He didn't know a man could be that scared and still breathe.

Jonah's safety, his very life, depended upon what Liam did next. Someone was trying to get to him, and if they hurt Jonah in the process, well, so much the better.

No!

Come after me, he wanted to shout. *Not my son.*

Only a coward would try to harm a child. Liam had plenty of experience in dealing with cowards, those who used the innocents of the world for their own vile purposes, warlords and insurgents who hid out in schools and hospitals, knowing that the American troops wouldn't attack.

A trickle of sweat worked its way down his back. He'd have decked anyone who called him a coward, but he was acting like one now.

He had to get Jonah somewhere safe, somewhere the people who were after Liam couldn't get to his son. The knowledge that someone wanted him dead and was willing to kill his son along with him shook him to the core.

Fear for his son hardened his resolve. Jonah had to be protected. At any cost.

Liam McKenzie didn't give in. And he didn't give up.

But right now he needed help in the worst way. Admitting he needed help didn't come easily. Not for Liam. Not for any special ops soldier who did his best to keep his country safe from the world's bullies. If keeping Jonah safe meant asking for it, then that's what he'd do.

He'd learned of S&J Security/Protection through buddies with whom he'd served. They hired ex–special operators, as well as former DEA, FBI, and ATF agents, like Paige Walker, the little sister of a friend from high school.

He called S&J and spoke to the founder Shelley Rabb Judd. "I need help," he said. After explaining his problem, he added, "I knew Paige Walker in high school. If she's available, I'd appreciate having her assigned to my case."

A pause. "I think we can arrange for Paige to help you."

Pride had no place when it came to keeping his son safe from harm. He'd ask for her help—he'd beg if necessary. Protecting Jonah was the only thing that mattered. Whatever the cost.

Paige Walker covertly studied S&J's newest client. Liam McKenzie. From the moment Shelley had given her the name, memories from fifteen years ago rushed back.

The jagged scar from a football injury in his senior year was still there, bisecting his left eyebrow. That captain-of-the-varsity-football-team face was even more handsome now. And the blue-green eyes were the same as those belonging to the boy she remembered, the boy she'd had a crush on so many years ago.

If the boy had been handsome, the man was now compelling. Crinkles at the corners of his eyes showed up white against a wind-scoured complexion, hinting at many hours spent outdoors. His once-blond hair had darkened to the color of wheat, and the planes and angles of his face had grown more defined. It was his eyes that had changed the most, though, holding both compassion and wisdom that had been lacking in the younger Liam.

She'd heard that he'd joined the army and had made

Delta, then started his own software company when he'd left the army. She watched as he scanned the room, dividing it into grids, she thought—a way of life for him, ex-Delta or not. The soldier was still in the man whether or not he wore the uniform. The stoic countenance and the quiet watchfulness were unmistakable.

To her mortification, her heart had picked up its beat, her breathing quickening. Could he detect the rapid rhythm of the pulse at the base of her neck? She was a professional, a trained agent. Agents didn't get all gooey-eyed over a long-ago crush. Agents didn't allow foolish schoolgirl feelings to interfere with work. Agents didn't feel any of the things she was feeling at this moment.

Enough.

Resolutely, she put the past where it belonged and prayed that her boss, Shelley, hadn't noticed her consternation. The last thing Paige wanted was for her boss to witness her acting unprofessionally. Her job at S&J Security/Protection was a safe haven in the chaos her life had become after she'd left the ATF.

So start acting like the operative you are and quit mooning about the past.

She listened as Liam recounted the last month and a half. Three of their former classmates had recently died in suspicious accidents. As soon as he mentioned their names, Paige knew the connection—they were all survivors of the bus crash that had killed her brother and four other students. When Liam added the attack on him and Jonah, she leaned forward.

"Where's Jonah now?" Paige asked.

"I took him to my parents' place in Savannah. He'll be safe there, and they love when he visits."

"Did you tell your parents what was going on?" Shelley asked.

"Only the bare bones. They knew something was up, but I didn't want to worry them more than was necessary."

He pinched the skin between his brows, released it. The small gesture was telling—he was worried but wanted to spare his parents the same. It reminded her of the boy she'd known from high school, the one who put others first. "What about the police? Have you told them?"

"I tried, but they brushed it off. I didn't have enough evidence—in fact, I don't have any at all—to prove that the deaths are related, much less murder. So far, everything has been made to look like an accident. One was a fall. Another died in a diving accident, and a third when an electrical short caused a fire in his house."

"The police didn't see the connection?" Shelley asked, a line forming between her brows.

"If I weren't part of it, I don't think *I'd* see the connection. Just three random accidents of people who happened to have been in the same class a decade and a half ago."

Would he share the details of that long-ago accident with Shelley?

"Fifteen years ago, I was in a school bus accident," he told Shelley. "The driver fell asleep, and the bus went over a bridge into a river. Five kids died. I was the strongest swimmer and, along with a couple of other boys, was able to save several kids, but we couldn't save everyone. I think this is payback."

"For you and the other survivors?" Shelley asked.

"It makes sense," Paige said.

Paige saw Liam's gaze on her. What did he want her to say? She couldn't fathom the expression in his eyes. "My brother died in the accident, too," she told Shelley. She'd never shared that with anyone at work. It was time she did.

Shelley reached for Paige's hand and gave it a gentle squeeze. "I'm so sorry."

"Can you help me?" he asked after a moment's pause. "Before anyone else dies." The words were choked out, causing Paige to wince in sympathy.

"You came to the right place, Mr. McKenzie." Shelley stood. "Paige is one of our best operatives. She'll keep you safe and help you figure out who's behind this." She turned to Paige. "Show Mr. McKenzie to your office. Come up with a plan and then get back to me."

Paige stood, as well. "Liam, come with me." Inside her office, she gestured to a chair. It was a bare-bones room, with little of herself in it. She liked it that way. At work, she wasn't reminded of the heartache of the past.

A utilitarian desk with one chair behind it and another in front plus a file cabinet were the only furnishings. She gestured to the uncomfortable-looking visitors' chair. The hard-backed chair minus cushions kept people from lingering.

Paige perched on the edge of the desk and gave him a moment to settle himself, taking the opportunity to study him. He hadn't changed much. Still drop-dead handsome. Still tall with the rangy good looks that had set most of the high school girls to daydreaming about him. His shoulders had broadened, his waist narrowed, the muscles hinted at in the boy he'd been more defined.

But if she were to point to the one thing that set him apart from the Liam McKenzie of fifteen years ago, it was his eyes. They were shadowed now, holding depths of hard-won experience and more than a little pain.

"Are you absolutely certain this is about the accident all those years ago? That's a long time to hold a grudge."

Even as she said the words, she recognized that fifteen years was nothing in the South, where memories were long with feuds dating back several generations.

"The deaths you've described are very different. I'm not saying you're mistaken," she said when he would have protested, "but it's a stretch. Statistically, in any group, you're going to have deaths, whether they be due to a fall or diving accident or a fire."

"There's a pattern here, outside the attack on me and my son," he insisted. "I know it. I feel it."

"We need more information, something that points to these deaths being related to the bus accident."

"If they're not related, I'm more at a loss than ever. But it's too much of a coincidence to believe that three of the survivors have died in the last six weeks unconnected with each other."

"Have any of the other survivors died? Or just those three?"

"Six weeks ago, Sam Newley died, but of natural causes. He had leukemia. It was only a matter of time. I attended the funeral, along with several others from my class." Liam shook his head several times as though to erase a painful memory. When he lifted his gaze to meet hers, his eyes were bleak. "Sam was a good guy, always looking for the best in others. I'm glad he can't see what's going on now."

Since Liam and the others of his class were five years older than her, she had to search her memory for a picture of Sam to bring up. Tall. Nerdy. Not handsome, but nice. "So, as far as you know, the others are still alive."

"That's right. With Sam gone and now these so-called accidents taking three others, that leaves six of us." A grim smile tipped his lips. "I don't want to wait around to see who's next."

"Are you close to any of the survivors?"

"We used to meet every so often. We vowed we would all do something important with our lives, a kind of pledge to honor those who died. For a while, we'd get together every year."

"That's great." For years after the accident, she'd longed to connect with someone who had been there with Brett during his last moments. Her parents had all but shut down emotionally after losing their only son. They'd refused to talk about Brett, refused to listen to her memories as she tried to keep him alive.

There'd been no time or patience for their daughter's tears and grief. Eventually, she'd learned to keep both to herself. Brett lived on because love lived on.

She'd loved her big brother with all her heart and still did. He had been not only her brother but also her best friend. Being two years younger than even the freshmen, she'd had little interaction with them. For the most part, they'd shunned her, treating her as an oddity at best, and, at worst, a pariah, one who skewed the curve with her remarkable mind.

But Brett had always been there, ready to listen when she poured out her loneliness, ready to take on anyone who mistreated her. Not many wanted to mess with one of the school's star football players, especially one who stood six feet two inches and came in at a hefty 190 pounds.

Normally easygoing, Brett had been fiercely protective of his little sister. Once, when some upperclassmen had backed her against a bank of lockers, calling her "Superbrain," he'd gotten in their faces and threatened to mop the floor with them. The message had been clear: you want to mess with my little sister, you'll have to go through me.

No one had ridiculed her again, at least not in Brett's hearing.

"Yeah. Too bad it didn't work out." The rueful tone of his voice told its own story.

"Let me guess. The group met for a few years and then everyone went their own way."

"Good guess. I still hear from some of them now and then, but everyone is busy with families, jobs. Life." He lifted a shoulder in a you-know-how-it-is shrug.

"That's natural."

Another shrug. "I stay in touch the best I can, but I'm a single parent with a business to run. Any spare time I have is spent with Jonah."

"You said your son was five? How did he take being sent to his grandparents?"

"He loves them, and they adore him. They couldn't be happier to have him."

A smile found purchase on her lips. "Do you have a picture of him?"

"Remember—you asked." He brought out his phone and scrolled through a couple of pictures. "Never ask a parent if they have pictures of their children. We could spend the next two hours going through them and still not scratch the surface."

The obvious love for his son warmed her. How cute was it that Liam, a former special ops soldier, like many of S&J's operatives, could show off pictures of his little boy with unabashed pride and such deep affection that it caused tears to prick her eyes? "You're a proud father. I get it."

"Being Jonah's dad is the best thing that's ever happened to me. If something were to happen to him…"

The words seemed to have stuck in his throat. To give

him time to compose himself, Paige looked away, once again touched by the father's love for his child.

"And I'm wasting time." The banter left his tone. "I need help, Paige. Your help."

"Why me?"

"Because you know the players. Or at least some of them."

"Correction—I knew the players. They were Brett's friends. They tolerated me hanging around, but mostly they considered me his bratty little sister, always pestering them. Plus they were three grades ahead of me."

"And five years older," he added.

"Don't remind me." Her grimace was heartfelt. "Going to high school at twelve was a mistake. My parents tried to tell me, but I insisted that I could handle it. I did all right academically, but I bombed socially. I never fit in. Brett always stood up for me." She gave a self-deprecatory laugh. "The teachers didn't know what to make of me, either. It didn't take long to figure out that I didn't belong, but I was too proud to admit it."

"If I remember correctly, you did more than all right academically. You graduated at fifteen with honors, then went on to Ole Miss to study law enforcement. Graduated with honors by the time you were seventeen."

Surprised and flattered that he knew this, she felt warm color rise to her cheeks and prayed Liam didn't notice. "How did you know? You were long gone by then."

"I kept tabs on you."

She stared at him. She'd never even thought Liam McKenzie knew her first name—she was always Brett's little sister—and now he told her that he'd kept tabs on her? It was both flattering and disconcerting. She wanted to ask how long he'd kept tabs on her but decided against it.

"Not in some stalkerish way," he hurried to add. "But your brother died in that accident. I wanted to know how you were doing."

She didn't respond immediately. How could she when she had no idea of what to say? She made a point not to look back on those years following the accident. They had passed in a blur of tears on her parents' part and guilt on her own—guilt that she was alive and Brett wasn't.

As far back as she could remember, she'd known that Brett was her parents' favorite. No matter what her accomplishments, she couldn't compete with the golden boy. For the most part, she'd been okay with it…until he died and she'd witnessed her parents' marriage slowly die along with him.

She'd attempted to take up the slack, had tried out for sports teams because that's what Brett had excelled at. Nothing she'd done had been enough, and in the end, she'd quit trying.

"Nothing was ever the same after Brett died," she said after a long pause. "Our family kept going. Sort of. My parents split up the year I graduated. With Brett gone and me leaving home, there was nothing to keep them together." She directed a knowing look his way. "What happened wasn't your fault. You did your best to save the other kids and got out as many as you could."

"I wish my best had been good enough. For Brett and the others."

His gaze darkened and locked with hers. Guilt had left a nasty stain upon the boy and the man. She wanted to tell him that guilt never solved anything.

She ought to know, but she couldn't give advice she'd never taken herself.

* * *

Liam hadn't made a mistake in coming here and enlisting Paige's help. She was still the same über-intelligent girl and straight shooter he remembered from high school. The girl who had once been all braces, elbows and knobby knees had grown into a breathtakingly beautiful woman.

Dark red hair, the color of fall leaves, framed a face dominated by high cheekbones and brown eyes with flecks of gold in them. She didn't try to play up her looks; on the contrary, she wore her hair pulled back in a ponytail, and her face was free of makeup. In his eyes, that made her all the more lovely. The appeal was unconventional and altogether unexpected.

Wow.

That had been his first thought.

His second was that he needed to keep his mind on business. He was a target. More importantly, he was all that Jonah had in the way of parents. His wife had taken off shortly after Jonah had been born and hadn't looked back. Whatever bitterness he'd once felt toward her had long since vanished. She'd given him the most precious of all gifts: his son.

For several years, he'd blamed himself for her desertion. Now he saw it for what it was: selfishness and insecurity on her part. She'd never wanted to be a mother, never wanted the whole family thing that had been his dream—a white picket fence and a big sloppy dog. His success with his software company had been the draw. If he hadn't been so caught up in his dream of home and family, he'd have seen that she was more interested in his money than in him.

He put aside any attraction he felt for Paige. He wasn't

going down that route again. The only thing he needed from her was to keep him and Jonah safe.

He felt like he'd traveled back in time. He'd spent the last fifteen years trying to forget, and now it was back. With a vengeance. Sometimes it was just too much trouble to keep the memories stored away where they couldn't hurt him. Sometimes it was best to let them have their way. It looked like this was going to be one of those times.

"Where do you want to start?" he asked.

"Back in Willow Springs. With the families of the kids who died. I'm assuming you have a list."

He opened his backpack, pulled out a tablet and showed her the list he'd compiled of kids who had died in the accident, their families, addresses and anything else he thought important.

She glanced at it. "Got it."

"Just like that?"

"Just like that." She tapped her temple. "Photographic memory."

"Must come in handy."

She flashed a grin. "Sometimes."

He shouldn't have been amazed, but she'd managed to surprise him all the same. "Any other superpowers you want to share with me?"

"I can't leap over buildings in a single bound yet, but I haven't ruled it out."

"Let me know when you take your first leap."

"You'll be the first to know."

In the parking lot, Liam pointed to his car, a navy Suburban. "I'll drive."

"Okay by me."

Liam pointed the car toward Willow Springs. He hadn't been back to his hometown since graduating from high school. When his parents had relocated to Savannah, there'd been no reason to return and plenty of reasons not to.

The trip took longer than it should have due to construction and detours. One detour took them deep into the country, where rolling hills and valleys replaced city streets and highways.

As they approached a particularly steep canyon, Liam applied the brakes. Nothing. He repeated the process, then pulled the emergency brake. Same result. He shifted the car into a different gear with the same result. Not only were the brakes out, the steering was gone, as well.

"What's happening?" Paige's voice was calm, though he heard the tension underlying the words.

"I don't have control of the car. I think someone's hacked into the operating system and taken it over." Liam did a quick scan of options, none of which he liked. "We have one shot at surviving. And it's a long one. When the car goes over the edge at the next curve—and it's going to—we have to jump. Tuck your head inside your arms and jump."

"Jump? You're kidding. Right?"

"I wish I were." He loosened his muscles and undid his seat belt. "Now!"

TWO

Paige jumped.

With her arms crossed over her face, she rolled down the rock-strewn cliff until a stubby tree halted her momentum. Rough bark bit into her arm. The wind knocked out of her, she held on, breathing heavily.

They'd both jumped just as the car went over the edge, Liam on the driver's side and she out the passenger side. The car tumbled down the side of the canyon and came to rest at the bottom with a crash of metal and glass.

She shuddered at what would have happened if she and Liam had still been in the car. If they hadn't jumped when they did, they'd undoubtedly be dead.

Liam. Was he all right? She looked about, spotted him about a dozen yards from her position.

"You okay?" he shouted.

"I think so." She'd be sporting plenty of bruises and scrapes, but nothing felt broken. She shook her head in an attempt to clear it and the ringing in her ears.

"Can you get up?" His voice echoed in the surrounding valleys and hills.

In answer, she braced her back against the tree and tried to stand, grateful to find that her legs were working. Barely. Her right shoulder and arm had taken the brunt of the impact with the tree, and she winced as she tried to move them.

"How are your climbing skills?" he asked.

"Let's find out." Now wasn't the time to tell him that she had an irrational fear of heights. *Don't look down. Keep focused on the next step.*

It was painstaking work, their progress measured in inches rather than feet as they clawed their way up the steep grade. Recent rains had turned the hillside into a muddy slide. With her bare hands, she scooped at the wet, crumbly dirt, seeking any handhold.

Kudzu vines covered the hillside, coiling and curling. She used them as anchors when there was nothing else to give her a firm hold.

Half-buried rocks tore at her palms, shredding the skin, but she didn't let the pain stop her. More than once, she lost her footing. Fortunately, she was able to grab onto something and didn't follow the path of the car.

Heavy winds whipped through the canyon, fighting her for every inch of progress. They stung her face and made seeing beyond her next handhold nearly impossible. Still, she kept climbing.

She refused to let wind, mud and gravity defeat her, but for every step she took forward, she slid back two. Fury at whoever had hacked into Liam's car propelled her forward when it would have been easier to give up.

"Need help?" Liam said when she stumbled for what seemed the hundredth time.

She was no rock climber, but she could handle this. Irked that he thought she couldn't, she said a curt, "No, thanks."

But her foot slipped as soon as the words were out. She grabbed the first thing within reach and found herself hanging from an offshoot of a tree, a flimsy thing when she thought of the distance to the bottom of the hill.

Suspended over the canyon, she clung to the branch for all she was worth. Slick with blood and mud, her hands slipped, and she doubled down on her grip. Another minute, two at the most, she'd lose her tenuous hold altogether or the branch would break beneath her weight. Either way, the consequences would be the same.

She struggled to steady her breathing. Hyperventilating wouldn't help.

Think.

But the silent command did little good when her heart was caught in her throat and her hands skidded farther and farther down the branch.

Thank You, Lord, for always being here for me. If this is it, I know You have another plan in store for me, something wonderful. I pray that I can be worthy of it. The silent prayer took hold in her heart and soothed the ragged edges of her fear.

The Lord was in charge.

Calmer now, she turned her focus to getting out of this. Depending upon the Lord was second nature, but she knew that He expected her to do her part.

"Hold on."

She turned her head to see Liam moving in her direction.

He came to a halt and clung to an impossibly narrow ledge. There were no further handholds for him to get closer. "Can you swing yourself over here?" He stretched out his arm.

"It's too far. I can't reach you."

"Jump. I'll catch you."

"Again with the jump?" she asked and made the mistake of looking down. The view stole her breath and her hard-won calm. Sweat formed at her temples, trickled down her cheeks onto her neck. She started to wipe it away and nearly laughed aloud at the absurdity of the idea. She was holding on for dear life and was troubled by a few droplets of sweat?

Get a grip, girl.

"Don't." The single word, barked in a loud voice, came out as a command. "Don't look down. Just jump toward me. I'll catch you. That's a promise."

When she hesitated, he said, "Look at me, Paige."

She did and saw the steady assurance in his eyes.

"I don't break my promises." He flashed a confident grin her way.

Could she do it?

Would Liam catch her?

Did she trust him with her life?

With a start, she realized that none of that mattered. The real question, the only question that truly mattered, was did she trust the Lord?

With a prayer on her lips, Paige jumped.

Again.

Liam caught her wrist and, for one breath-stealing moment, she dangled over the canyon. Buffeting winds sent her swaying back and forth, anchored only by Liam's hand.

Veins protruded from his heavily muscled arm as he took her weight. With a grunt of effort, he swung her to the narrow ledge where he stood. He shifted so that she faced the earthen wall, sheltering her from the wind with his body.

Her heart did a series of somersaults as she realized how close she'd come to dying. The Lord, with Liam's help, had saved her.

"It's okay." The words whispered against her neck, and she shivered in response.

"Thank you," she said when she found her voice, though it came out as a croak. She tried again. "Thank you."

"Catch your breath, then go ahead of me," he said. "I'll be right behind you."

The last thing she wanted to do was to start up the cliff again. They had at least fifty feet to go. Could she do it?

"We'll make it," he said.

"Another promise?"

"Yeah. And I always keep my promises."

With painstaking care, she reached for a tree root, grabbed on and pulled herself up. Another step. When she felt like she couldn't lift her arms one more time, Liam encouraged her.

"You can do it. I know it."

She reached the top and collapsed on the rough ground. So grateful that she was still in one piece, she scarcely noticed the rocks poking through the thin cotton of her shirt or that her arm ached unbearably. With what seemed monumental effort, she rolled over and stared up at the sky. The blue had never looked more blue, the clouds never more billowy.

Liam knelt over her. "You were great back there."

"Not so great. If it hadn't been for you…" She shuddered at what would have happened.

He stood, then reached out a hand to pull her up. "You'd have figured it out. You're too stubborn to let a little bitty hill get the best of you." The teasing note in his voice was softened by the warmth of his eyes as they rested on her.

She choked out a laugh. "Little bitty hill?"

"Sure. Compared to the mountains in Afghanistan, that one was little bitty."

"If you say so." A smile tugged at her lips, then disappeared as she considered their circumstances. At the same time, another spear of pain radiated through her arm. The grimace that escaped her lips had Liam frowning.

"What's going on?"

"My arm got banged up a little. No big deal."

"Let me have a look." Gently, he probed her arm and shoulder. "It's not broken, but it's pretty badly sprained." At her look of surprise, he said, "I had some medic training. Not a lot but enough to recognize the difference between a break and a sprain." He tore off a sleeve from his shirt and used it to fashion a crude sling. "That should do for now."

"You're a good guy to have around in an emergency."

Liam gave a mock bow. "Aw, shucks, ma'am. Ain't nothin'."

She grinned at the exaggerated accent.

"Now, if only I could sprout wings," he added, "I'd fly us out of here."

Once again, she smiled in appreciation of his humor. The truth was, though, there was little to laugh about in their situation. The wind picked up, and she shivered in clothes wet with mud.

"We're stuck in the middle of nowhere, and I'm guessing we don't have cell coverage." She let her gaze travel over the sweep of earth and sky. The beauty of God's creations never failed to move her, but the mountains and valleys didn't make for good cell reception.

She said as much to Liam, causing him to pull his phone from his pocket. "You're right."

"I wish I wasn't." She looked around, got her bearings. "The highway should be about five miles east. We'd best start walking."

He looked down at her shoes. "That's another thing I remember about you. Sensible shoes. Even in high school."

She followed his gaze to her well-worn high-tops in hot pink, her favorite color. Right now, she could have used a pair of hiking boots, but the sneakers would have to do. "I never saw the point of wearing shoes that you can't walk in."

With that, she took point and prayed her sense of direction wouldn't lead them wrong.

So many things could have happened in the last few minutes. She and Liam could have been killed as they jumped from the car. They could have been seriously injured. Other motorists could have been killed as the car careened down the highway.

But none of that had happened.

Thanks to the Lord. She recognized His hand in saving them. She said a silent prayer in her heart, knowing that the Lord heard every prayer, however it was uttered.

She slanted a glance Liam's way. She longed to urge him to give thanks for their safety, but she didn't.

He would undoubtedly take it as preaching, and that was the last thing she wanted to do. To her mind, preaching defeated the purpose of bearing testimony of the Lord's love, so she remained silent.

Gratitude to the Lord couldn't be forced. It had to be freely given, as was His love. She wished she could convince Liam of that and that she could share with him the healing balm of His care.

Liam's gaze rested on her. "Your eyes reveal your every feeling."

His words startled her from her musings.

"What do you mean?"

"Right now, you were giving thanks to the Savior that we came through this with our skins intact. You're also wondering why I don't feel the same."

"None of my business."

His short nod of acknowledgment confirmed her suspicions about his feelings if she were to share her faith in the Lord right now. "Thank you for not preaching to me."

"That's not my job. Besides, preaching doesn't work."

"No. It doesn't." He let the subject go. "You're very transparent. How did you ever make it in the DEA? Isn't there a lot of undercover work?"

She ignored the last question and focused on the first. "How did you—" She stopped. Of course he would know what she'd done before joining S&J. He'd mentioned that he'd followed her career. In addition, her background was posted on the company's website.

If he'd done more digging, he would have learned that her fiancé had died on her last operation with the ATF. And that it had been her fault. A picture of Ethan Stockton, his body bloodied and broken, flashed in her mind. With the resolve of long practice, she willed it away.

But there was no censure in Liam's expression. Only sincere interest. She didn't pursue the opening he'd inadvertently provided about not being a believer. She had too many secrets of her own to pry into those of others.

Liam wasn't surprised that Paige had been praying. Nor did he begrudge her faith. He only wished he still believed. As a child, he'd gone to church every week with his parents. While they had listened to the preacher's message, he'd attended Sunday school. He'd continued attending church until the day that everything had changed forever.

He could no longer believe in a God who had allowed five young people to die so senselessly. The feeling was only confirmed when he'd observed what he had in Afghanistan. Brutality, on both sides, didn't begin to describe the horrific acts he'd witnessed.

Whatever remained of his faith had vanished.

Paige had handled herself like a pro on the cliff side. She'd been scared—who wouldn't be—but she'd done what was necessary.

He wasn't sure what to make of her. She was beautiful, smart and courageous, but there was a shadow in her eyes that spoke of pain. Was she still grieving for her brother? It was possible, but he sensed it was something more.

Now wasn't the time to probe. Nor were the shadows in her eyes any of his business. Once this was over, they'd go their own ways, she back to S&J and he…well…he might be taking a different path from running the software company. Taking a job with the US Marshals was looking more and more appealing. He wanted to make a difference in the world. Maybe serving with the Marshals was the way to do it.

He checked his phone and found that he had reception. "We're in range."

"I'll call S&J. They'll bring us wheels."

Within twenty minutes, two burly SUVs appeared. A giant of a man stepped out of one. Liam gaped, recognizing the man at once.

Raphael Zuniga, known as Rafe the Strafe to those in the special ops community, reached out to clasp Liam's hand. "I heard you were a client."

Liam did his best not to wince when Rafe shook his hand. Though Liam was in no way small, his hand was dwarfed by the larger man's. The two had served together in Afghanistan years earlier. A mutual respect had developed, along with a healthy appreciation for each other's abilities, but Liam readily admitted that he was outclassed by Rafe, who stood six feet five inches and came in at a hefty 250.

Rafe had a reputation for having a soft heart when it came to kids and animals. Otherwise, watch out. He was a force to be reckoned with, and his reputation among the spec ops community and the enemy had grown until it had taken on legend status. A modest man, he'd been largely unaware of it, making him all the more likable.

Paige stepped forward. "Thanks, Rafe." She nodded to a second man, who climbed out of the other vehicle. "And the big man himself. Jake Rabb, meet Liam McKenzie."

Liam studied the cofounder of S&J with interest. Shelley Rabb Judd and Jake Rabb had built the firm from a modest two-person operation to one that was now internationally recognized with offices all over the Southeast and in a couple of other countries. "Thanks for helping us out," he said, his nod including both men.

"No problem." Jake tossed a set of keys to Paige. "You okay?" he asked, eyeing her arm with concern.

"Nothing a bath and clean clothes won't take care of."

"Heard you had a little problem."

"You could say that. We almost ended up at the bottom of a canyon, along with Liam's car."

Rafe raised his eyebrows. "What've you gotten yourself into?" he asked, looking first at Paige and then at Liam.

Liam quickly outlined what had brought him to S&J. "Paige is helping me sort through it."

"If anybody can do that, it's Paige." Jake winked at her, then his expression sobered. "Do you need backup?"

"We're handling it." She turned toward Liam. "Let's go back to the office and get cleaned up. Then I want to find out who hacked your car." Determination vibrated in every word.

Liam slammed a fist into his palm, the smacking sound mimicking what he'd like to do to the men who had hacked his car. "And tried to kill us."

THREE

Four hours later, after a trip to the hospital, where Paige's arm was put in a proper sling, and a shower and change of clothes, Liam and she were once more on the way to Willow Springs. The SUV belonging to S&J was a powerhouse, and they made the trip without incident.

Before leaving the office, Paige had set up a program to trace the hack into Liam's car's operating system. If they were fortunate, the program would give them a username. In the meantime, they had work to do.

Liam was more grateful than ever that he'd sought help from S&J. Paige had jumped right in and made his fight hers.

"Cheer up," she said as she navigated the congested roads out of the city. "We're making progress."

"How do you figure?"

"Someone tried to kill us. That means he's running scared."

Liam snorted, thinking Paige had a strange idea of progress. "Whoever it is already tried to kill me. Forgive me if I don't see a second attempt as progress."

The pessimistic outlook wasn't like him, but two attempts on his life in only a couple of days tended to take the humor right out of a person.

"But this time he didn't try to make it look like an accident. The hacking is traceable. It's provable," she said. "We've got something to take to the police when we decide to involve them, which I hope is sooner rather than later." An earlier attempt to tell the police what he suspected was met with outright disbelief.

"You're right. On both counts. Maybe there's a way to put an end to this before anyone else has to die." He shoved a hand through his hair. "You're pretty great, you know that?"

"How so?"

"You jump from a speeding car. You get tossed down the side of a cliff. You climb your way out with a sprained arm. And you don't complain. Not once."

"I was complaining plenty when the ER doctor decided I needed a tetanus shot."

"You scared of a needle?"

"Not much. Well," she amended, "maybe a little. And it was a really big needle."

He laughed. "In that case, your fear is perfectly justified."

"That looks good on you," she said.

Some of the tension fell away from him, and he felt more like the young boy he'd once been, ready to take on the world.

Reality intruded far too quickly, though, reminding him that he was no longer that idealistic boy, certain he could change the world for the better. He had seen too much of the world's violence and hatred and had come away sobered by the ugliness he'd witnessed. Waging war on those who preyed on his country and other freedom-loving countries had made him stronger, but it had also stripped away his innocence.

"What?" he asked.

"Laughter."

"There hasn't been much to laugh about lately."

"No, I guess there hasn't."

Paige was quiet after that, her profile in repose, giving him the opportunity to notice the soft line of her cheek, the firm set of her jaw.

No woman had truly caught his interest since his wife had left him and Jonah. Though he'd dated a few times, he'd only been going through the motions. There'd never been a second date.

He kept his mind on the trip to his hometown and did his best to keep it off the very appealing Paige Walker.

The small town located west of Atlanta's sprawl hadn't changed much since Liam had left it fifteen years ago.

Memories too powerful to deny crowded his mind. Though Willow Springs was only a scant twelve miles from Atlanta, it might as well have been twelve hundred in terms of growth and progress.

Two white clapboard churches stood as sentinels on either end of Main Street. A dress store advertising "ladies' fine apparel" occupied a small storefront, flanked on one side by the town's only barbershop and on the other by the VFW. Veterans and nonveterans alike congregated outside, always ready to swap a tale that grew with each telling.

Liam recalled that, according to his father, his grandfather had marched in the town's first veterans' parade celebrating the end of WWII.

It was a good town. Or it had been. The accident had claimed more than five lives—it had claimed much of the town's spirit, as well. The high school graduation that year had been subdued, the celebratory air associated with such events conspicuously absent. Everyone had done what they could to bring a festive note to the occasion, but the effort hadn't been enough. In the end, the graduation ceremony had been cut short, even the mayor's normally robust speech unable to rouse the newly minted graduates and their guests.

"It hasn't changed much, has it?"

Paige's question penetrated the murky mire of the past. "No."

"I've been back a few times," she said, surprising him. "I wanted to see if it was like I remembered."

"What did you decide?"

"On the outside, yes. But the feeling was different. It was as though the town and everyone in it were only going through the motions."

That mirrored his own thoughts. "I remember a headline from right after it happened. 'Bus accident claims five of Willow Springs' finest and brightest.' Every time I went out, I felt like people were pointing to me and whispering, 'He's the one that let our kids drown.'"

"Could be that's you projecting your own feelings. What I heard is that you were a hero. And that's what I told anyone who said different."

"You were in the minority then."

Paige reached for his hand, giving it a quick squeeze. Though she didn't say anything, the simple gesture warmed him through and through. When she released his hand, he felt the loss.

They began with the family of Liam's best friend, Danny Howard. The two had competed in football and basketball and just about everything else and had come out at the end closer than ever. Far from resenting the competition, they'd used it to be their best.

Danny had been good-natured and an admitted class clown. College hadn't been in his future, and he'd accepted that, always planning on going into the army. It hadn't taken a degree in psychology to know that was why Liam had entered the army shortly after graduating from college with a degree in engineering. Honoring Danny's memory that way was the only thing Liam had been able to do for his friend. Plus, he had desperately wanted to make a difference in the world, to protect his country, as both his father and his grandfather had done.

The exterior of the house was as he remembered. Neat. Well maintained. Until he looked more closely. Chipped paint around the door. Piles of rotting leaves left unraked. Mr. Howard had once been fanatic about keeping up the house and yard.

Liam didn't want to believe that his friend's parents had anything to do with the so-called accidents. The Howard family had been a second home to him, Mr. and Mrs. Howard another set of parents. He'd tried to keep in touch, but when his letters had been returned unopened, he realized that the relationship he'd once cherished had died along with his friend.

Danny's father opened the door to their knock. He recognized Liam immediately. "McKenzie. What are you doing here?" The gruff voice was not at all what Liam had remembered of his friend's father. Nor was the combative stance of arms folded across his chest and legs spread, firmly planted.

"Mr. Howard. It's good to see you." Liam introduced Paige to his friend's father, who ignored her and fixed his gaze on Liam.

"Why are you here? We've got nothing to say to each other."

"Mr. Howard," Liam tried again, "I need to talk with you. If you could spare us a few moments of your time—"

He opened the door and pointed to two chairs. "Say

what you're going to say and get out. I've got no use for you. No use at all."

Liam and Paige each took a seat. He gave a thumb-nail sketch of the accidents that had claimed three lives.

But the older man didn't seem to be listening and ignored Liam's explanation for the reason of the visit. "You and Danny were best friends," he said. "How could you have let him die like that?" Accusation and grief warred in the man's voice, the years in no way softening either.

Liam understood both, had felt the biting sting of accusation and the bruising pain of grief himself. Now he attempted to give that understanding to a man who glared at him with soul-piercing contempt.

"I'm sorry, Mr. Howard. Sorrier than I can say. If I could have saved Danny, I would have. I'd have given my right arm for him, as I know he would've for me."

Liam's failure to save his best friend still ate away at his soul in the dark corners of the night. When the driver fell asleep, the back end of the bus was hit because he was swerving. Rosemary had been trapped by the damage, and the others had convinced Liam to go for help because he was the strongest swimmer. They'd said that they would free their friend and be right behind him. Liam had done as they'd urged.

When it was all over, many had blamed Liam for not staying behind to help free Rosemary, claiming his added strength could have helped save her and his closest friends. If only he'd been quicker, stronger, smarter and gotten back to them sooner. If only…

"You have a strange way of showing it, coming here and accusing me of what…killing three people and then trying to kill you?" The man's mouth stitched tight on the last word.

It turned out he'd been listening after all.

"That's not what we're saying," Paige said, speaking for the first time. "We're trying to find out who's picking off the survivors and put a stop to it. We thought you might have some ideas."

"You'll get no help from me. Good riddance to them, I say." He clasped his hands together, wrung them, then looked down at them as though he didn't know how they'd ended up in his lap.

They were a workman's hands, Liam reflected, the knuckles swollen, scars bisecting his fingers and palms, evidence of a lifetime of working construction. Danny used to say that his father didn't know the meaning of leisure time, that work and more work were all he'd ever known, all he'd ever wanted.

Shame washed over the older man's face. "I didn't mean—" He shook his head, the gesture one of defeat and sorrow rather than anger. "I don't know what I mean anymore."

"Harold?" A thin voice came from the other room. "Do we have company?"

The man disappeared from the front room.

Liam heard the murmur of voices from an adjoining room. One, Mrs. Howard's, was faint and querulous, the other, her husband's, patient and soothing. He tried to hear the words but couldn't make out more than a few.

Mr. Howard returned shortly. "Excuse me, but I have to see to my wife."

"Is she ill?" Paige asked.

"She has early-onset Alzheimer's. Doctors say it might have been brought on by stress." Howard aimed a hard look at Liam. "Like losing her only child when he might have been saved. After Danny died, she was never the same. I lost my son and my wife that day." He covered his face with his hands, and his thin shoulders heaved with a gut-wrenching sob. "Nothing was ever right again."

"I'm sorry, Mr. Howard," Liam said and stood. "I'm sorry for your loss." Danny's death had weighed heavily on Liam. It still did. His friend had been in the back of the bus, along with Brett, two of the cheerleaders, Rosemary and Torrie, and Liam's own girlfriend, Marie. Though Liam had made repeated trips back to the bus, swimming through the murky river water, he'd been unable to reach them. And they'd refused to leave Rosemary behind to save themselves.

Whenever he was in the States in between deployments, he made a trip to the cemetery on the anniversary of the accident and laid flowers on the graves. He tried to time his visits when no one else was there. The last thing he'd wanted was to run into grieving family members.

"Which one?"

"Both."

"Do me a favor and get out. Don't come back. For both our sakes." For a moment, his gaze softened and he resembled the easygoing, kind man Liam had known so many years ago. "Please." The plea in his voice nearly ripped out Liam's heart.

Paige remained silent as she and Liam returned to the car. "I'm sorry," she said when they reached the vehicle.

"For what?"

"For what he said to you. He didn't have any right to say what he did."

"He has reason to hate me." Liam unlocked the car but didn't get in. He braced his hands against the car door and stared into space. "If I'd been faster, stronger, smarter, maybe I could have saved Danny, Marie, Brett, Rosemary and Torrie."

"And maybe you wouldn't have been able to save someone else. Mr. Howard's wrong. And so are you if you keep blaming yourself." She wet her lips, working to find the courage to say what she wanted to, needed to. "I lost my brother in the accident. I know what grief feels like, but I never blamed you."

She didn't open the car door immediately. Instead, she folded her arms across the roof of the car. "You have to know that you did everything you could. I could see it in your face at the funerals."

On the other side of the car, Liam mirrored her.

She remembered the funerals. Five. Four friends and one very dear brother buried. Five lives taken. Five families destroyed.

"What did you see?"

"Pain. Unspeakable pain. I knew at the service for Brett that you wished it had been you. I wanted to tell you then that it wasn't your fault, but my parents needed me at their side."

"And they wouldn't have taken it kindly if you'd tried to comfort the boy who had let their only son die. They made their feelings plain to me that day."

"They were so filled with grief that they were incoherent."

"What about you? You were grieving, too."

"I was. But it wasn't the same as what my parents were going through. You have to understand. Brett was their golden child. The star athlete who went to state and was going to have a brilliant career as a pro football player after he graduated from college. After…after the accident, Mom put away all of Brett's trophies. She said she was decluttering, but I knew she couldn't bear to look at them anymore. Dad just stopped talking. Not to Mom. Not to me. Not to anybody."

"They must have been proud of you, too. You weren't exactly chopped liver."

Her lips pulled into a self-deprecating line. "My parents loved me, but they never knew what to do with me. I was too different. They didn't know what to make of a child who started high school at twelve and college at fifteen. If I had been athletic or popular like Brett was, it would have been better."

"For who?"

"For them. They looked at me and saw this geeky girl who didn't fit anywhere."

"What about now? Do you see them often?"

"They each remarried, have new families. I have two half-brothers. My parents and I see each other once every couple of years or so. It's not perfect, but it works." She gave him a probing gaze. "Enough about me. You think those deaths were your fault. They're not. They never were."

"Look, I appreciate what you're trying to do. You're right—it wasn't my fault, but sometimes it feels like it." Another sigh that was more a huff of grief. "Like now."

Paige made to speak, but he cut her off with a hard thrust of his hand. "Don't. Just…don't. When I was in the Stand, our unit took fire from enemy insurgents. We were outnumbered by a factor of two. Yet I sent three men, three good men, on a reconnaissance mission to scout out an alternative route. Two were killed. One returned with the information I needed. I sent those men to their deaths. Our unit escaped. Barely.

"Afterward, I was presented with a medal. I told my CO that I didn't deserve it. I'll never forget what he said. 'Son, you're not getting a medal for what you did but for having to live with it.' I didn't understand what he meant then, but, later, I did. It's the same with the kids in the bus. I had to live with it. All of it."

She leveled a steady look at him, telling him that she disagreed with his self-blame but that she wouldn't argue with him anymore.

He turned the conversation back to business. "I think we can cross Mr. and Mrs. Howard off our list."

Paige slid in behind the steering wheel.

Before she had even buckled her seat belt, she heard a distinctive click.

"Don't move," he warned.

Paige stilled. Didn't dare breathe. Sweat slicked her forehead, gathered above her upper lip and dampened her underarms. But she was cold. So cold.

That was what intense fear did to you. It had you sweating bullets while, at the same time, turning you extremely cold.

Goose bumps prickled her arms, causing her to shiver.
Do. Not. Move.

The silent order stiffened her backbone. She wasn't a simpering miss. She didn't scream at the sight of a cockroach the size of a drone. She didn't scream if she came across a snake. She refused to scream just because there was a bomb placed under her seat.

"Did you hear it?" he asked.

She gave a tiny nod, afraid to move, afraid to breathe. How long could she hold her breath?

Not long enough.

"I hope I'm wrong," Liam said, "but it sounded like the click a pressure plate gives off when it's activated."

She'd learned about pressure plates while working for the ATF. Some of the crime families used them to take out rivals or even agents, but she'd never come up close and personal with one.

"I think you're sitting on a pressure plate."

She worked to keep the panic out of her voice. Breathe. Release. Breathe. Release.

"They're a favorite of terrorists in the Middle East. Don't move," he said again.

"Wasn't planning on it."

"Good. I'm going to bend down, check out what we're dealing with. If it's what I'm thinking, we're going to have to do some strategizing."

"Like calling in the police?"

"We'll do that. But we don't have time for them to get here."

"This just keeps getting better and better." The panic was coming back.

"That it does, but I've got some experience in defusing these bad boys."

"Good to know."

He looked up, gave her the same grin he had on the cliff. "We'll get through this."

"Is this another one of your famous promises?"

He didn't answer, instead looked at her right arm trussed up in a sling. "This is going to be a little tricky."

She'd already figured that out. She also knew that she couldn't allow him to risk his life for her. He had a son who needed him. "You ought to get out of here. Wait for the police, the bomb squad. No sense in both of us—" She didn't finish. She didn't have to.

The grim line of Liam's lips told her what he thought of her suggestion.

"You think I'd leave you?" Outrage rimmed every syllable.

No. She didn't. Afraid to say anything more, she shook her head. At the same time, she bit down on her lip. Hard. The pain gave her something to focus on rather than the fear that crawled up her spine to settle at the base of her neck.

Buck up, girl. You've faced down terrorists, gunrunners and smugglers. What's one bomb?

He rounded the car to her side. "On the count of three, be ready."

"For what?"

"This." With that, he grabbed her good arm and yanked her from the seat before she knew what was happening.

FOUR

Liam pulled Paige from the car and half dragged, half carried her away from it just as it exploded. He sheltered her from the pieces of metal and debris raining down upon them by hunching over her. Shards of glass pierced his neck and hands, but he scarcely noticed.

Protecting Paige was instinctive. He didn't think about it. He just did it.

The acrid stench of smoke, gasoline and burning metal singed the air, stinging his eyes and nostrils. He blinked rapidly, trying to clear his vision.

Sirens sounded in the distance. Someone had already called 911.

When the aftershocks of the explosion came to an end, he rolled off her and hunkered at her side. He brushed soot from her face. "Are you okay?"

She looked dazed but nodded. "What about you?" She didn't give him time to answer as she brushed glass from his hair and aimed a reproving look his way. "You cheated—you didn't count to three."

He knew she was trying to lighten the atmosphere and appreciated the effort. *What a woman.* They'd nearly been killed—again—and she was doing her best to reassure him that she was all right by making light of the fact that someone had tried to blow them up.

"That's what you have to say after we were almost turned into mincemeat?" He held out a hand to help her up.

"That and thank you." Her voice shook, then steadied. "That's twice that you've saved my life. I owe you." She accepted his hand and stood, lips pulled in a rueful line. "I'm supposed to be protecting you."

"The next one's on you."

"The next one? I'm hoping there won't be any more. I still say you cheated." The teasing note in her voice defused much of the remaining tension that roiled through him.

Liam played along. "My humblest apologies." Thinking of what might have happened, he sobered. "I didn't want you tensing up when I pulled you from the car."

"I got that. You could have taken off and saved yourself."

He rolled his lips inward. "Not my style."

"I know."

He saw the effort it was costing Paige to hold herself together, but she didn't give in to tears. He'd witnessed battle-hardened soldiers break down in tears after a near miss in the field and didn't hold it against them. Just as he wouldn't have held it against Paige if she'd given way to tears, but she held steady.

He was learning that that was who she was.

The warmth in her gaze as it rested on him had Liam feeling like a schoolboy after stealing his first kiss. It was gratitude Paige was experiencing, nothing else. He'd do well to remember that.

As she started to comb her fingers through her hair, he caught her hand and stilled it. A piece of glass was lodged against her temple. With exquisite care, he removed it before she cut herself.

Her eyes met his. "Thank you. Again."

An ambulance arrived. He and Paige were examined, their cuts and scrapes treated. Both refused to go to the hospital for a more thorough examination.

By that time, curious onlookers had gathered behind the crime scene tape. It had always annoyed and even angered Liam that people considered an accident or a crime a source of entertainment, delighting in the misfortunes and tragedies of others.

Mr. Howard stood on his front porch, studying the scene. He shook his head and went back inside his house.

Liam didn't expect anything more.

The next twenty minutes were spent being quizzed by the police. Uniforms did the initial questioning before a detective showed up.

A fireplug of a man, he stuck out a beefy hand. "Reineke."

After shaking it, Liam introduced himself and Paige and submitted to yet more questions.

No, they didn't know who had set the explosion.

No, they hadn't seen anyone suspicious.

No, they hadn't noticed anyone following them.

The interrogation continued until Liam had had enough. "Maybe if the police had paid attention when I told you about the so-called accidents, this wouldn't have happened."

"You should have come to us sooner."

"I did." Liam put some bite in his voice. "I went to the Atlanta police, and no one believed me."

The detective's expression edged toward apologetic.

"That's on all of us who wear blue, but the Willow Springs PD will take a long look at things." His voice hardened. "We want you and Ms. Walker to come in and tell us what you know."

"We'll be there."

"Now." Any sign of contrition vanished as the detective folded his arms across a bulldog chest.

"First," Liam said, "we need to see about getting some new wheels."

"Make it today." Reineke huffed out an impatient breath before stalking off.

"A real people pleaser," Paige said.

"Yeah. He's a charmer, all right."

A rueful smile pulled at Paige's mouth. "S&J isn't going to be thrilled with me for totaling a car."

Liam grimaced at the thought of reporting his own totaled vehicle. "I'm sure not making myself popular with my insurance agency, either."

They arranged for another car at a rental place to be delivered there. Forty-five minutes later, they took delivery of the vehicle.

"Good choice with the full insurance package," Paige said, tongue in check.

Liam gave a mock growl. "Seemed like a good idea at the time," he said and drove to the police station.

The station house smelled of sweat, anxiety and bad coffee.

There, they asked for Detective Reineke and were ushered to his office.

The detective stood and pointed to two hard-backed metal chairs that were obviously not designed for long-winded visitors. "Tell me everything. From the beginning. Don't leave anything out."

His brusque manner and clipped voice were hardly inviting, but Liam complied and laid out what he knew, starting with the school bus accident fifteen years ago, then the first alleged accident that had taken place six weeks earlier. "His name was Bryce Mendenhall. He died in a fall from an apartment balcony. I didn't think much about it except for regretting that I hadn't stayed in touch better with someone who used to be a friend."

"He was a player on the football team you mentioned, is that right?" Reineke asked.

"Right. Then the second accident happened, a diving accident. This time it was Angie Raul. She was a cheerleader. And then a third, Roger Newsom, who died in a house fire caused by an electrical short. By that time, I knew something was off and started paying attention. That's when I went to the Atlanta police. Two days ago, my son and I were nearly run off the road. I took him to my parents' in Savannah, then came back and contacted S&J Security/Protection."

"Which is when you entered the picture," the detective said with a brief nod in Paige's direction. "I'm familiar with your firm. It's got a good rep."

"Thanks." Her nod was equally crisp. "We've been interviewing families of the kids who died in the accident. So far we haven't turned up anything, but there's no doubt that someone is trying to stop us. Full disclosure—my brother was one of the kids who died in the accident."

Reineke chewed on his lip as he digested that. "Do you have a list of families of the survivors?" the detective asked. "We'll want to run our own investigation, but it may be that the bus accident had nothing to do with what's going on now."

Liam ground his teeth, letting his glare do the talking

for him. When he finally trusted himself to speak, it was with undisguised disgust. "You've got to be kidding."

"There could be other reasons someone wants you dead. And we've yet to prove that those accidents that claimed the lives of your classmates were murder." Impatience nipped at the detective's voice. "We've got to check every angle."

"And what happens while you're checking those angles? Three people have died so far. And three attempts have been made on my life. Three for three. I'd say that covers all the important angles. Don't you see?" Urgency roughened his voice. "Someone is killing everyone who survived that accident. Three people have died. How many more deaths do you have to have before you see the truth?"

"Look at it from my perspective," the detective said. "You just brought this to us, and now you want us to jump on it when, in your own words, you have no proof."

"Nothing else makes sense."

"Accidents happen all the time. To all sorts of people. Why not to a few of the survivors of this accident you keep going on about? Statistically speaking, it's unlikely to happen so close together, but it's not out of reason."

"Three in six weeks strains the law of averages, doesn't it?"

"I don't know. Does it?" The detective left the question standing. He gave a pointed glance toward the clock, then slid the thick folder back across his desk to Liam. "You've put together quite a file here. Three deaths. Three attempts on your life. What I don't see is any similarity between the attacks. Murderers usually stick to a script once they find one that works. These killings, if that's what they are, are all over the place."

"The fact that they are made to look like accidents is the pattern," Paige pointed out.

The detective made an impatient gesture. "I get that. Tell me why," he said, directing a hard stare at first Paige and then Liam, "these accidents are occurring now." He rubbed a hand over his jaw.

"That's what we haven't figured out," Liam admitted. "The only thing that's changed in the last six weeks is that one of my friends died, this time of natural causes." He explained about Sam Newley passing away from leukemia.

Reineke shoved a hand through thinning salt-and-pepper hair that was already standing on end. "I don't see the connection."

"Neither do we." Liam's admission came after a long breath.

"I'm willing to believe there is a connection. I'm just having a hard time seeing it. I wasn't here when the accident happened, but I know about it. Way I heard it, it was about the biggest thing to ever happen in Willow Springs." He turned to Paige. "Ms. Walker, what do you think?"

"I trust Liam's instincts."

Liam flashed her a grateful smile.

"We'll do a deep run on Newley," Reineke said. "See what we can find out. Let's go back to the beginning. You say fifteen years have gone by since the bus accident. That's a long time to hold a grudge."

"I'm guessing by your accent that you're not from around here," Paige said, raising a surprised expression on the detective's face.

His voice with its distinctive Northeastern inflection and hard consonants stuck out. "Yeah. What about it?"

He didn't give them the opportunity to answer. "Boston. What does that have to do with anything?"

"This is the South," Paige said. "Fifteen years is nothing." She snapped her fingers. "It's less than nothing. Memories tend to run long here."

"So I'm learning." Impatience was now replaced with frustration. The detective looked at his notes before rubbing a hand over the bald spot on his head. So agitated was the motion that Liam wondered if he'd rubbed the hair right off at some earlier time. "Can I keep this folder? I assume you've made copies."

Liam nodded.

"I have your contact information. The two of you, try to stay out of trouble."

To Liam's ear, the words held more warning than concern. "We didn't go looking for it." He stood and let his ramrod posture answer the implied warning. "But I'm not walking away from it."

Silence stretched between the two men, along with a hard look. Soldier to cop.

A heavy sigh caused Reineke's chest to heave. "Didn't think you would. But I had to say it."

"I'm not dropping this," Liam emphasized.

"For your own safety..." Reineke flushed as he pulled out words that were reminiscent of old television cop shows.

"For my own safety, I have to keep at it. No offense, Detective, but for you, this is just another case. For me, it's my life and my child's life. You could say that I've got a vested interest in seeing this through."

"I can't stop you, but I can warn you not to step on anyone's toes."

"We're going to be doing a lot more than stepping on

toes by the time this is done." Liam turned on his heel and walked out the door.

He'd do what he had to do. Nothing more. Nothing less.

Outside, Paige struggled to keep up with Liam as he walked off his mad. His long legs ate up the sidewalk with angry strides.

She'd recognized the signals he was giving off in the police station—the straightened spine, the tension rolling off him in almost palpable waves, the rigid line of his shoulders.

"Hey, hold up," she called when he gave no indication of slowing down.

He paused, waited while she caught up. "Sorry." He kept walking, albeit at a slower pace.

Sensing his need to think things through, she remained silent until he started talking.

"For a little while there, I thought we were getting somewhere," he muttered. "A few days ago, they wouldn't give me the time of day, shook me off like I was some kind of crackpot conspiracy theorist. Now Reineke *says* he's going to look into it, but he still doesn't really believe that the accidents are connected. My guess? He'll just go through the motions."

"Maybe in going through the motions, he'll turn up something we've missed."

"Not unless he starts seeing this for what it is. Revenge killings. It can't be anything else."

He was right. The police seemed reluctant to connect the attempts on Liam's life with the three so-called accidents and with the bus accident of all those years ago. She supposed the police had to be cautious in jumping to conclusions, but, for her, the time for caution had passed.

People had died and more were likely to unless she and Liam found out who was behind this.

"I don't think we're making friends in the police department," she said. "Of course, that's just me."

His lips quirked. "Yeah. I got that impression, too."

"When this is over, I'm going to have to make some amends. S&J likes to keep a good relationship with the police. It comes in handy."

"When this is over, I'll help you. But right now, I'm more interested in finding out who's trying to kill me and the others." Regret showed in his eyes. "And now I've gotten you involved in it. You didn't sign up to ride in a hacked car, dangle from a cliff and almost get blown up all within a day. If you want to cut me loose, I wouldn't blame you."

"Not my style," she said, repeating his words of a short while ago. "I'm with you."

He gave her a long look that had her wanting to squirm beneath its intensity. "Thanks. That means a lot." Then, as though that shared moment had never happened, he said, "Let's head to my place. I want to show you something."

Paige looked down at her torn and bloody clothes. She hadn't taken the time to change after the explosion. "I'll meet you there. I want to go home and get cleaned up." She made a face. "Hanging around with you is hard on a girl's wardrobe."

Liam glanced down at his own clothes. "An hour sound okay?"

"Perfect."

As Paige drove home, she received a call from the IT specialist at S&J. Though Liam's car's operating system had clearly been hacked, there was no way to trace it. So much for that lead.

At home, she showered and dressed in fresh clothes. There was nothing like a hot shower and clean clothes to make a woman feel better. She tossed the clothes she'd worn in the trash. There was no way they could be salvaged. She decided she didn't need the sling anymore and tossed it, as well.

She dried her hair, touched her lips with gloss and decided she'd do. Liam hadn't hired a glamorous model. He'd hired a trained operative, and that's what he'd get.

Head in the game was what she needed. Anything else was off the table.

Liam studied the two whiteboards he had been keeping for the last month. On it were pictures of the victims, the survivors and the bus driver, with family members of each. Notes were scrawled beneath each picture with arrows connecting individuals to each other.

Above each picture was a label. Accidental. Natural. Homicide. Living. A map was taped to a second board, detailing where the victims had died, complete with names, dates and times. A drowning death at a beach. A short circuit resulting in a house fire. A fall from an apartment balcony. Three very different kinds of deaths, ruled accidents by the authorities.

But he knew better.

When he found proof, those labels would switch to homicide. Even if the police didn't buy in to the theory, he knew it. He felt it in his gut, and he trusted it just as he had while leading his unit in Afghanistan. Call it instinct or intuition or whatever—it had never let him down.

Should he remove the pictures of the survivors' family members? No way would they be involved in the deaths. They understood just how precious those lives were.

He shook his head in answer to his question. Those

families were part of the whole, and if he was going to understand what was going on, he needed to see the whole of it.

Maybe if he mixed up the pictures, moved those of the victims and interspersed them with the remaining survivors?

He put thought to action, but the new juxtaposition didn't shake anything loose. What wasn't he seeing? He knew it was there, if only he were smart enough to make sense of it.

He and Paige had stumbled onto something yesterday. The killer was no longer trying to make it look like an accident.

Mentally he retraced their steps. First to Danny's parents. There was open hostility from Mr. Howard, but Liam didn't peg him as the killer. Grief over his son and then his wife had clouded his mind, but he wasn't a murderer.

Nothing there.

Then…what?

It couldn't go on. It wasn't just his life, but those of the other survivors. It occurred to him that there were now two classifications of survivors—those of the original accident and those remaining after three had recently died. Four, he corrected himself. Sam Newley, too, was one of the original survivors.

What was Sam's place in this? Logic said he didn't have one. He'd died before the first accident/murder took place.

Liam had put up a picture of Sam, anyway. As an afterthought, he'd included Sam's younger brother. It wouldn't hurt to pay him a visit. Maybe Sam had said something to his brother before his death that would jog a memory loose in Liam's mind. At this point, he was willing to try anything.

Though he'd talked with most of the other survivors about whether anyone had been following them or had tried to harm them, he'd come up empty and had only succeeded in scaring them. He couldn't regret it, though. They were right to be scared. Maybe that would cause them to take extra precautions.

The pictures started to blur. His thoughts cycled over and over, a loop he seemed unable to break. What wasn't he seeing?

The question tormented him until he turned his back to the board and pressed his fingers to his temples. The right piece in the right place would explain everything, only he wasn't seeing it.

If only he could remember something, anything, to make sense of what was happening. He pulled out a notebook and pen from his desk. Computers were great, but sometimes writing things out helped to clarify them. He'd done the same when he was faced with a problem while serving in Delta.

He started with the morning of the accident. Methodically, he went through the events of getting ready. Having the breakfast he didn't want but that his mother insisted he eat. Driving to school. Attending the pep rally before the game. Exchanging high fives with the players and other students. Eating lunch in the cafeteria because there wasn't time to go off campus. And then the bus ride to the game.

What had he been wearing? Oh yeah. His letterman sweater. That was a given, even though it had been far too hot for the heavy garment on a day where the humidity and the temperature each topped eighty-five. Khakis. An off-brand pair of sneakers because his parents couldn't afford a name brand and refused to buy him a pair despite his claims that everyone was wearing them. That had been a sore spot between them.

Looking back, he wondered why it had been so important that he wear a trendy pair of sneakers. Remembered shame filled him as he recalled the hot words he'd shouted to his mother and father for not giving in to his demands. He'd been unbearably arrogant and now marveled they'd ever put up with him.

Nothing was too small to overlook, so he recorded everything, even his capitulation on removing his sweater, acknowledging that it really was too hot.

He described each of the kids on the bus in as much detail as he could summon. Snippets of conversation appeared in his mind, and he transcribed them to paper as accurately as he could.

He shook his head as he called up the foolish dialogue that went on between his teammates and the cheerleaders. Light flirting mixed with some bruised feelings when a warm smile wasn't returned or a coy flip of the hair was ignored. The players were full of themselves, and the girls responded to the bravado of boys feeling their way toward manhood.

Harmless fun. Nothing more.

He continued with his note taking, including the locker room chatter, the good-natured ribbing between the boys about who would score the most points on the field, the game itself, the after-game blow-by-blow account.

And then the ride home.

The excitement of winning the final game of the season. More high fives of buddies congratulating each other and themselves. The excited hum of the cheerleaders, just as thrilled over the score as the players. The promise of a celebratory dinner for just Marie and him.

Everything had been so normal.

Until the bus ran off the bridge and his world had changed forever.

"What am I missing?" The question, directed to the empty room, remained without an answer.

Paige was due to arrive in a few minutes. He'd invite her in, show her the boards, get her take on them. She had a good eye. Maybe she would see what he was missing.

The thought of Paige had his lips curving in a smile. Brett's little sister had grown up into a beautiful woman.

Liam pushed back the thought. He needed to get his head in the game and off Paige Walker. His life and those of others depended on him doing just that.

FIVE

Paige arrived and was let in by a distracted Liam.

"Come on back."

A family room, kitchen and dining area combined to make a great room that had Paige envious of the space and the air of casual comfort it promised. Put-your-feet-up furniture and practical hardwood floors said the home was designed for living, not just for show.

Family pictures and what must be the art projects of a five-year-old covered every surface and most of the walls. She wanted to linger over the pictures to absorb the obvious love that existed between Liam and his son, who was blond-haired and looked seriously adorable with an off-center dimple in his chin.

A brightly colored poster caught her attention. A mother bird watched over her babies with the caption *What if I fall? Oh, but, my darling, what if you fly?* The gentle encouragement in the words caused a pang to settle in her chest as she thought of her relationship with her own parents. They hadn't so much discouraged her as they had forgotten her. That was somehow worse.

The hurt no longer crippled her as it once had. Now it was only a sore place in her heart, one that had healed but remained tender in the harsh light of examination. She doubted Liam's son ever felt discouraged or forgotten.

The sense of home here, the comfort and coziness of it, wrapped her in a warm blanket—one she longed to snuggle up in and close out the cares of the day.

Her two-bedroom apartment, littered with moving boxes yet to be unpacked and nothing personal but for a single African violet on a windowsill, looked cold and sterile by comparison. She'd lived there for over a year and had made only half-hearted inroads into settling in.

She had reasons—legitimate reasons, she told herself—why she hadn't done more than the minimal amount of unpacking. She'd dug through a few boxes as she'd needed items, but aside from a few feeble attempts, she'd done little to turn the apartment into anything but a place to sleep and change clothes.

Work came first. And when she returned home from work, she was exhausted, far too tired to tackle the chore of opening boxes and deciding where to put things.

Also, she wasn't sure she was going to keep the apartment for very long. Why bother unpacking only to go through the whole process again? she asked herself, conveniently ignoring the fact that she'd been there well over a year now. She recognized the reasons for the excuses they were. In truth, she hadn't done more because the apartment wasn't home and never would be.

She'd worked hard to make a home in her condo in Virginia, where she'd been based with the ATF, as she and Ethan had planned to live there after they were married. After he'd died, she knew she couldn't stay. She'd sold the condo, resigned from her job, and moved to Atlanta for a new job and a new life. She had the job, but her life was in a holding pattern she felt powerless to break.

Liam looked at her strangely. "You okay?"

Startled, she realized she'd lost herself in the past. "What? Oh yeah. Fine. I was just admiring your home. It's beautiful."

He glanced around as though seeing the room for the first time. "Hardly beautiful. But it suits Jonah and me." He gestured to the sofa, where dents in the cushions bore evidence of it being well used. "I'm not much of a decorator. My ex-wife wanted everything perfect, but I'm more of the lived-in style."

"Me, too." She took a final look around. "Beautiful," she repeated, more to herself than to him, and then gave a slight shake of her head, clearing it. She'd spent enough time mooning over what she didn't have. It was time to get to work.

"This is how I've been spending my time," Liam said and gestured to two huge whiteboards set up by a bank of windows.

Pictures of the bus accident victims and survivors, along with family members, covered one board.

"What do you see?" he asked, then quickly covered his mouth as a yawn escaped.

She glanced at him and frowned.

Dark crescents underscored the bleakness of his eyes, and the skin stretched tighter across his cheekbones. He looked totally drained.

"How much sleep have you gotten in the last few days?" she asked.

"I don't know. A few hours here and there."

"You won't be any good to yourself or to the investigation if you don't get some shut-eye."

Anger flashed in his eyes before he gave a jerky nod. "I hear you. Humor me for now and tell me what you see. Then I'll get some sleep. I promise."

"I'm holding you to it." She studied the board again.

"Connections. You and Marie. Marie and Reva. Brett and Rosemary. Sam off by himself. Mr. Pope, the driver. You probably know that he died last year." She took two steps back, cocked her head at a different angle, hoping for a new take on the pictures. "What I don't see is how they help us discover who's doing this."

"Me, either. The pieces are there. And so is the answer. I feel it in my gut. I just don't have them in the right places yet. If I juggle them into different places—" he moved the pictures around "—they still aren't telling me anything."

She tucked her thumbs in the back pockets of her jeans and rocked back on her heels. "Like a jigsaw puzzle."

"Just like."

"Maybe we aren't asking the right questions." Another rock back on her heels. At the same time, she rolled her bottom lip inward and caught it between her teeth.

"What do you mean?"

"We've been asking who has reason to kill the survivors."

Liam's nod was thoughtful. "What should we be asking?"

"Maybe we should ask ourselves why now. Why did the killings start when they did, and what secret is someone trying to hide? This is more than just killing off those who got out of the bus that day. If that were the case, the killings would have started a lot sooner."

She spoke slowly as the theory took shape in her mind. "Something's changed. Something important enough that makes it imperative the survivors be eliminated. If we knew what that something was, we'd be a lot closer to finding the killer.

"Why now?" she asked again. "After fifteen years, why start killing the survivors now?" She circled back to the idea of secrets. "Secrets have a way of coming out no matter how deeply they're buried. We discover that secret, we find the killer." She said it with more certainty this time.

Liam reached out to brush an errant strand of hair from her face.

She started at his touch.

"I'm sorry," he said and withdrew his hand quickly. "I didn't mean to startle you."

"You didn't." That wasn't strictly true. His touch *had* startled her, but not for the reason he thought.

Since Ethan's death, she'd worked alongside men. The accidental brush of an arm or a hand had left her unmoved. So why did Liam's touch evoke such a reaction?

It made no sense. No sense at all.

With herculean effort, she pushed away the feelings and focused on the job. She kept coming back to the same question. What had happened in the years between the accident and now to make someone want to kill off the survivors?

She and Liam bounced theories back and forth, but none felt right. Most people didn't murder without a reason. Even psychopaths had a reason, even if it was one only they could understand.

"Your theory about a secret would explain why the killings started now, rather than five, ten or fifteen years ago." He went quiet, and she knew he was rolling it around in his mind. "Lots of people have a secret or two in their past, something they'd prefer others not know, but a secret worth killing for? Something that big takes it to a whole new level."

"That's why it's so important you think back on that day. Something happened. Something besides the accident."

"Something bigger than five kids dying?" Skepticism was heavy in his voice.

"Maybe something that points to the reason the bus driver fell asleep at that moment." She pulled up memories of that time. "Pope was never charged, though plenty of people were clamoring for just that, including my parents. They wrote letters to the district attorney and demanded he be held accountable, but nothing ever came of it. I remember feeling sorry for his wife and son."

"They left him," Liam said. "I can't say that I blame them. And we can't escape the fact that he was to blame for the bus going off the bridge. He fell asleep. It wasn't like he set out to kill anyone, but he was responsible. Your idea about a secret is a good one, but I don't see where this is leading."

Discouragement settled in as she accepted the truth of that. Her theory that someone was killing off the survivors to keep a secret was just that: a theory. She had nothing to back it up. Nothing but a hunch. Cases were built on irrefutable evidence.

"I see you included the bus driver's family. Why don't we pay them a visit tomorrow? His wife or son might remember something of that day."

"Why don't we?"

Mindful of the time and his promise to get some sleep, she said, "Time for me to leave. Can I take a picture of the boards before I go? I want to study them at home."

"Go ahead."

Using her cell phone, she took pictures of the two boards. "I'll see you tomorrow morning."

At home, she looked over the pictures again. Nothing popped.

The following morning, Paige and Liam were on their way to the last known address of the bus driver's wife and son. A little digging revealed that the driver's wife had taken their then twelve-year-old son and left her husband shortly after the accident.

It couldn't have been easy for them, Liam reflected. Calvin Pope had been regarded as the villain of the piece and had taken the brunt of blame for the deaths. Though he hadn't been charged with a crime, it had been close. In the end, the city prosecutor had decided that a trial would only prolong the suffering and pain of those families who had lost a child. No evidence had come to light that he had planned the accident. Driver error was the consensus, a tragic accident with deadly consequences.

Though there was no law against drowsy driving in the state, civil cases had been brought by two families of the kids who'd died. The other three families, including Paige's, had elected not to go that route, deciding not to prolong the agony. The juries had ultimately ruled against the families, creating more bitterness, more pain.

As Liam followed GPS directions to Pope's wife's house, he noted the increasingly run-down conditions of the community as they neared the address. The neighborhood had obviously not been on the receiving end of city funds intended for the gentrification that was sweeping through much of the area. Overgrown grass and cars set up on blocks in front yards composed much of the landscaping. Every once in a while, a pot of flowers sat on a stoop, a valiant effort to bring some color to the dreariness of the neighborhood.

Graffiti warred with gang symbols on walls and garage doors. More often than not, the gang symbols won, a silent testament that violence had more than a toehold in the community.

He kept his weapon close at hand.

"What happened to Pope's wife and son that they had

to move here?" Liam wondered aloud, though he could guess the answer.

"Fallout from the bus accident."

"Of course."

The Pope home wasn't the worst on the street, but it came close.

"I don't mind saying that I'm glad we're both carrying," Liam said, narrowed gaze taking in the surroundings.

The house bearing the address of Pope's wife and son hunched over, as though it had been beaten down by despair. Like the rest of the neighborhood, the dwelling might have been attractive at one time. The simple design with large windows and a deeply pitched roof hinted at good bones, but it had peeling paint, missing shingles and cracked windows.

Kudzu grew with wild abandon around the cement foundation, while ivy made its way up the crumbling brick exterior and air-potato vines dripped from the porch eves.

Liam gave a firm rap on the door.

A woman who looked like she could be anywhere between fifty and eighty greeted them with an unsmiling mouth. Hair that might once have been light brown was a dull gray, and it framed a thin face tight with harshly carved lines that spoke of a joyless existence.

Like the house, Mrs. Pope hunched over, as if she, too, had been beaten up by life. She held the door open a few grudging inches and lifted a scowling face at them.

"I'm not buying nothing, so don't waste your breath trying to sell me something I don't need. I don't have money for useless stuff that just takes up space."

"That's good," Liam said, "because we're not selling anything." He quickly introduced himself and Paige before the woman could slam the door in their faces and explained about the accidents that had brought them there. "We're hoping you can help us make sense of what's happening," he concluded.

"Come on in, if you have to."

As though in afterthought, she pointed to a couple of chairs. "Sit down if you've a mind to. But don't be expecting me to entertain you or nothing. I've got better things to do with my time."

She pointed to the young man slouched against the wall. "That's my son, Cal Jr." His posture shouted boredom, but the expression in his eyes was one of sharp interest.

To prove her point, she picked up a newspaper and cracked it open. She squinted at the paper—not surprising since the room seemed shrouded in darkness.

Liam glanced at the two windows and saw veils of vines obscuring much of the light. He shifted his gaze to the one piece in the room that spoke of happier times: a photograph of a school class with printing announcing it was Mrs. Fletcher's sixth grade.

"Mrs. Pope, if you could just give us a few minutes of your time," Liam began.

"I don't know why you're here. Me and my boy don't have nothing to do with them accidents."

"I'm sure you don't," he said in a placating manner.

She lifted her head and glared at him. "So why are you here if you don't think we had anything to do with what's happening? And it's Hawkins now. I dropped the Pope a long time ago. I don't need the bad history it carried. I have enough problems without carrying around the misery of the past."

"Mrs. Hawkins," Paige said, trying again, "do you have any idea of who might want the survivors of that day dead? You have a unique perspective, being the wife of the driver and not a member of any of the families who lost someone."

The woman snapped the paper shut and leaned in, eyes hot with resentment. There was an eagerness to her, like she had been waiting for the right audience upon which to air her grievances. "Who'd want those kids dead? You mean 'sides me?"

"What do you mean by that?" Liam asked.

"I mean that accident destroyed our lives. It tore our family apart and left us broke and homeless. Me, Cal Jr. and Calvin himself. He might as well have died, too, for all the good his being alive did us. Him passing away last year was a blessing. It surely was. Least he had a bit of life insurance for Cal Jr."

"Five families lost a child," Liam said, striving for neutral. "Surely you haven't suffered more than they have." What kind of woman compared herself to those families who endured such a horrific event as losing a beloved child?

The older woman sneered at Liam and then Paige. "You think you're so high and mighty, Mr. Liam McKenzie and Ms. Paige Walker." She fixed her gaze on Paige. "I remember you, all right. You didn't belong in high school any more than a one-eyed goat did. My Calvin came home and laughed at you, trying to fit in with all those kids so much older than yourself. He called you a poseur. What good did it do you anyway?"

Liam wanted to defend Paige from the attack, but he didn't know what to say. He glanced at her, saw that she was holding herself calmly under the attack.

Mrs. Hawkins continued with her tirade, shaking her finger with such vigor that her whole body quivered. "I know you lost a brother, one of those glory hounds on the football team, full of themselves. But you didn't lose your whole life. That's what happened to my boy and me. Look around. What do you see?"

She gestured to the cluttered room with its peeling paint, cracks in the walls and water stains on the ceiling. "Junior and I moved here after that first year. People in Willow Springs turned mean. Real mean. Blamed Calvin for what happened. I admit he wasn't much, but he put food on the table and kept a roof over our heads. I never had no education. Married Calvin at seventeen and never did graduate high school."

A brief smile softened her face, giving Liam a glimpse of the girl she'd once been. "We were in love and ready to take on the world no matter what our parents said. I always wanted to go back to school or get my GED at least, but Calvin…he wanted me home." The smile died. "He did his best to take care of us, I'll give him that. Maybe it was his fault he fell asleep on the bus, but was that any reason to run me and Junior out of town? We didn't do nothin' wrong."

Liam started to say something, but Mrs. Hawkins wasn't finished.

"I won't deny that Calvin could be lazy, but a woman can't be held responsible for what her man does, can she? It wasn't fair. Not fair at all. I know what you kids called Calvin. Old Goat Pope. He pretended that it didn't bother him none. But I know it did. He did his job and that was that. You kids just had to torment him, didn't you? You had no call to do that. 'Course after the accident, he didn't have a job. That day changed everything."

"For a lot of people," Liam said.

Mrs. Hawkins sat back, flipped open another tabloid with enough energy to cause it to tear. "Now look what you made me do. I wanted to read what's happening over there in England with those royals. Their shenanigans make for a good story, even if I've got no truck with them. Bunch of spoiled brats with too much money and not enough work to keep 'em out of trouble, if you ask me."

Clearly, the woman didn't expect a response to her rantings. And Liam wondered, what was there to say? Pope's wife blamed everyone else for her circumstances. She was so caught up in her own misery that she couldn't see beyond it to what was happening outside her own narrow-minded world.

"What happened to your husband after the accident?" Liam asked.

Mrs. Hawkins spat out something that Liam decided he was better off not hearing. "What do you think? Calvin lost his job and the puny benefits that came with it. He was called a murderer. People wanted someone to blame, and he was a handy target. The school board fired him. There was talk about arresting him and making him stand trial. Like he wanted those kids who thought they were so high and mighty to die. He didn't have any liking for them, but he didn't wish them dead."

Liam flinched at the spiteful words. He tried to feel sorry for the woman, but Mrs. Hawkins's hostility made it hard to summon up much sympathy. "You sound angry."

Hawkins pointed at Liam with a bony finger, accusation rigid in every inch of her posture. "'Course I'm angry. Angry at you."

Taken aback by the attack, he only stared at her.

"You're angry at Mr. McKenzie for saving your husband's life?" Paige asked, voicing the same question Liam had.

"I heard you were smart. Turns out you ain't so smart after all. He should have let Calvin die."

Her son pushed himself off the wall where he'd been

leaning. "Ma, don't be saying those things. You'll give folks the wrong idea."

"I don't care what idea they got. Truth's truth. I won't apologize for it." Arms folded across her chest, she sat back, anger vibrating from her entire being.

"You can't mean you'd prefer your husband had died," Paige said, horror deepening her voice.

"Mean it? Of course I mean it. I mean it as much as I've meant anything in my life. If Cal had drowned along with those kids, it would have been different." A self-righteous sniff punctuated the words. "I'd have collected on his insurance. It wasn't much, but it'd have been enough to keep me and my boy going at least for a few years without me working myself into an early grave. I cleaned office buildings until my hands were callused and my fingers bloody. I got to where I couldn't do the work anymore, so now I'm on disability. Scrubbing floors and toilets is hard on the body, but it was the only job I could get. Nobody wanted to hire the wife of the man who killed five kids."

Gone was any semblance of civility as venom continued to spew from her. Harsh color stained her cheeks, and she aimed her rage at first Paige, then Liam. "When I found out what had happened, I was furious. If Cal had died trying to rescue those kids, he would have been called a hero. Instead, he was the man who had killed five spoiled brats.

"Thanks to your man here," she said, returning her attention to Paige, "Cal lived, so he was the villain. The rest of you got butter-wouldn't-melt-in-the-mouth sympathy from the whole town. People couldn't do enough for you. All I got were mean words and nasty looks. Someone even threw rocks through our windows. I ask you, did I deserve that?"

Liam wasn't given time to react to the words about his and Paige's relationship as the woman continued with her diatribe, repeating her words as though they were a kind of mantra.

"We were all tarred with the same brush. It got to where I couldn't go to the store to buy eggs without people thumbing their noses at me."

She pointed to the door. "Now, get on your way, both of you. We've got nothing here for you." Another spiteful glare at Liam and then Paige. "Yes, I knew the Walkers, knew that they saw trash whenever they looked at me. Your ma always looked like she'd been crying, like it was *my* fault somehow. I don't know anything. Anything at all. And even if I did, I wouldn't be sharing with the likes of you."

Liam shook his head when Paige would have protested and cupped her elbow. "Let's go. There's nothing to learn here."

To their surprise, Cal Jr. followed them out to the enclosed porch. "Don't pay no mind to Ma. She says a lot of things, but that's all it is. Just talk. She wouldn't hurt anybody."

"Are you sure about that?" Liam challenged. "She sounded pretty certain in what she was saying, blaming us and the rest of the survivors for what's happened to her, to you."

The man's face hardened. "Sure as I am that she can't drive. I take her everywhere. Ma wasn't lying about being disabled. She can barely make it from the bedroom to the kitchen without falling. I've picked her up off the floor enough times to know she's not faking it.

"If she were out trying to kill people, I'd know about it. I do my best to take care of her, but she's gone sour inside. Real sour. For your own good, don't come back."

He held the porch door open and waited pointedly until they stepped through it. "I don't expect to see you again."

Outside, the wind snapped with a mighty energy, the keening edge of it sharp against the skin, but Liam scarcely noticed. He was still ensnared in the hatred he'd seen in Mrs. Hawkins's eyes, a hatred so intense that it bored a hole into him.

What had he and Paige done to merit such loathing? He had saved the woman's husband's life, and all she wanted to do was to blame him for ruining her own. Hawkins's son was right: she had gone sour inside. Could that turn her into a killer? Could she and her son be in on it together?

Neither one of them appeared to have the cunning to carry off murders designed to look like accidents, but looks could be deceiving.

Liam held her car door open for Paige. When they pulled away from the house with its grim atmosphere and inhospitable occupants, it was with relief. Mrs. Hawkins's accusations pierced his soul. Though he knew he didn't deserve the condemnation the woman had leveled at him, Liam couldn't deny the dark feelings that swept through him.

He chewed on the idea that mother and son were behind the killings. Could it be? The son hadn't seemed hostile except toward the end, but he might just be more adept at hiding his feelings than his mother.

He shared his thoughts with Paige.

"Mother-son killing teams aren't common, but they're not unheard of," she said, her tone pensive.

The dilapidated house was filled with bitter grudges and black moods. Did it also hold a pair of murderers?

SIX

"We opened a can of worms back there," Liam said.

"And then some," Paige said as they lingered over coffee after a home-style meal of meat loaf and mashed potatoes at a corner diner. "My grandmother used to say that about people who'd made themselves particularly unwelcome."

They sat side by side in a booth, both with their backs to the wall. Paige never sat any other way and figured it was the same with Liam.

The diner was one of those places where red vinyl stools were pushed up to gray Formica counters and the same red vinyl covered the booths. The Formica was chipped and the vinyl cracked, which added to the vintage feel of the place. The food wasn't fancy and suited Paige just fine.

The homey meal had settled some of the hard feelings that the visit to the bus driver's wife had stirred up. Equally disturbing was Mrs. Hawkins's referring to Liam as *her man*. Granted, Paige liked Liam, admired him even, but she certainly didn't claim any relationship beyond client and operator with him. She sneaked a glance at him and hoped he had ignored the woman's words.

"I'd say *unwelcome* was putting a positive spin on

it," Liam said. "Mrs. Pope—or Hawkins as she goes by now—made it clear she couldn't get rid of us fast enough."

"Except when she wanted an audience for her complaints," Paige added.

"Yeah. She's got that down to an art, doesn't she?"

"She's so bitter over the accident, yet she didn't lose anyone. Seems the only thing she lost that she really cared about was her husband's paycheck." Paige acknowledged that she'd taken some hits from the woman's comments and was perhaps judging her overly harshly. Liam, though, had taken the brunt of it. He didn't deserve the charges she'd leveled at him.

As she pondered the question if Hawkins could be behind the murders, she couldn't make the pieces fit. The woman had been openly hostile. Would she have shown her hand that way if she were responsible for the killings?

Sharing her thoughts with Liam, she said, "Could she be cunning enough to let us see how much she hated the survivors in the hope that we'd dismiss her?" She shook her head to her own question. "I don't see her as that devious, as disagreeable as she is. Honestly, I don't think she has the brains to pull off killing three people and make it look like accidents."

"What about Cal Jr.?" Liam asked. "Could he have planned it? He was quiet until the end, but there was plenty of anger in him when he told us not to come back."

"He looked like he has his hands full just taking care of his mother. I have to give him props for putting up with her. It can't be easy living with someone so knotted up in anger and self-pity."

"She got to me," Liam admitted, his frustration evident in the crumpling and uncrumpling of his paper napkin until it was nothing but shreds. "I knew the families who lost kids blamed me, but I didn't expect it from her. I even thought she might be a little thankful that I'd saved her husband's life." His laugh was hollow. "Seems like I messed up a lot of people's lives that day, some I'm only finding out about now."

Paige reached out and stilled his hand in hers. When he withdrew, she knew a sharp sense of loss. Well, what had she expected? He didn't want solace from her; he wanted results.

"You know better than to take anything she said personally. She wanted someone to blame, and you were handy. It's as simple as that." Paige didn't doubt that if Mr. Pope had died, his wife would have blamed Liam for that, too. She was one of those unhappy individuals who was always looking to lay guilt on someone else so she didn't have to deal with the consequences of her own choices.

"She took some shots at me, too," Paige reminded him. "I can't say they didn't sting, but I'm not going to waste a minute worrying over them. My grandmother would say her heart's as sour as a lemon that's sat too long in the sun."

"Your grandmother sounds like quite a woman."

"She was. After the accident, I spent a lot of time with her, even lived with her for a while. She knew how things were at home and did her best to make it up to me. When she died last year, I felt like I'd lost my best friend. My parents didn't come to the funeral. They were busy with their new families, so it was just me and my friends from S&J there to mourn her."

Grief ambushed her, and tears leaked from the corners of her eyes. "Sorry about that," she said, knuckling away the errant tears. "I don't usually cry like that."

"No, I don't guess you do." This time, it was Liam who took her hand in his and gave it a gentle squeeze.

The warmth of his hand was comforting. Too comforting. *Put it away.* She needed to keep things on a professional level. Hadn't she just reminded herself that the only thing that could exist between Liam and herself was a business relationship?

The reminder, though, did little to ease the zing of attraction his touch sparked. As unobtrusively as possible, she removed her hand from his.

After pushing her dishes to the side, Paige propped her elbows on the table and rested her chin on her folded hands. "Let's start back at the beginning. Tell me everything you remember about the day of the accident."

"I spent years trying to forget that day."

"It's important. Go back in time and try to remember. No detail is too small."

"Okay," he said, voice unutterably weary. "I'll do my best." He paused as he picked his way through memories.

A small smile kicked up the corners of his lips. "I remember Brett sitting by Rosemary Wilkins on the bus trying to sweet-talk her into going out with him the next night, telling her that he was the only man for her. Rosemary was flirting back, flipping her hair over her shoulder, smiling at him, the way girls do. Nothing serious, just playing along. I remember thinking that prom was only a few weeks away and that he was looking for a date. He had a way with the girls. I was envious over that."

"That was Brett," Paige agreed. "Always the flirt. He had a thing for Rosemary, but he liked a lot of girls back then, and they liked him back. What else?"

"Marie was talking to me, telling me about the new dress she'd bought for the senior prom and how I needed to get her a corsage to match it. Blue, I think it was. I remember sort of zoning out." He gave a sheepish look. "Guys don't care about dresses, you know. We look like we're interested, but we're not. I pretended like I was paying attention, but I was really going over the game in my head, replaying it, wondering if I could have made that last pass if I'd put a spin on the ball."

"Brett used to tell me the same thing when girls started talking about dresses. Anything else?"

"There was Sam Newley. He never said much, but when he did, you tended to listen." Liam's expression turned thoughtful. "He was always quiet, but on the way back, he got real still, sort of watchful, like he was waiting for something. I remember wondering what was making him so skittish-looking and left Marie to check on him, but he just shook his head. I finally gave up and went up front. I wanted to talk with the coach about the game. Then everything went wrong.

"One minute we're riding along just fine, and the next, we're falling off the bridge. It happened so fast that nobody knew what was going on. In a couple of minutes—or maybe it was seconds—we were underwater. We didn't have time to react except to panic. Everybody started scrambling for the exit doors, but they wouldn't open. I used my elbow to break a window near the front door and managed to get out that way. Once I was out, I opened the doors. Kids started pushing their way out, but the bus kept sinking. Our coach was knocked out, but another kid and I managed to get him to the surface."

Paige shuddered inwardly, thinking of the absolute terror that Brett and the others must have experienced. She wanted to tell Liam to stop, but she didn't. She needed to hear this as much as he needed to say it. For too long, she'd avoided the day that her brother had died. Now it was time to face it.

"People were trying to scream, but they couldn't." Liam's voice grew hoarse, as though the words were stuck inside and could only escape if he pushed them out one at a time with a great effort.

Paige kept her voice soft. "What happened next?"

"Some of the kids got out on their own. I tried to get to Marie, but I couldn't reach the back. Danny and Brett called out that Rosemary was trapped and the emergency door wouldn't open. They told me to save the others and get help. They'd all work together to get her out. Pope was blocking the front exit. He was really out of it, couldn't seem to make his arms and legs work. I remember wondering if he was sick. I had to get him out before I could rescue any of the others. I got him and some of the other kids to the surface, thinking I could get to Marie if they weren't in the way."

He choked over the words, cleared his throat and continued, "I went back for her, only by that time the bus had shifted, filling the back end with water. I can still see the look on her face. She knew she was going to die and I couldn't do anything to stop it. I remember Brett and Danny trying to push the girls forward, to get them out, but it was too late. Eventually, divers went back for the bodies." His shrug was eloquent with pain. "Those that made it out were all taken to the hospital, the rest... you know."

She knew all too well. The bodies had been taken to the morgue. As much as she'd tried to put that memory away, it was all too vivid in her mind.

Two police officers had made notification visits. She remembered the tortured grief in her parents' eyes upon learning of Brett's death. Her mother had given an anguished scream, her father shaking his head in denial.

They'd had to go to the morgue to make the identification. Up until then, her parents had clung to a desperate hope that Brett wasn't among the dead. The reality had sent them into a chasm of grief that had swallowed them in darkness. Uncontrollable sobbing on her mother's part and tight-lipped silence on her father's.

In the end it had been her grandmother and Paige who had seen to the funeral arrangements, making the necessary decisions, from choosing the coffin and the flower spray to be laid on top of it to the suit Brett would be laid out in.

She'd done her best, had supported her parents in every way she knew how, but it hadn't been enough. Nothing had been enough. Still, the grief was almost better than the vacant expressions both wore as life without Brett set in. They'd moved through the house like shadows. Her mother's skin had been so translucent that Paige imagined she could pass her hand through it.

All the while, she'd tucked away her own grief, burying it deep inside her heart where no one could see. When her parents had praised her strength, she'd basked in the rarely given compliment.

She'd taken over the running of the household, had made certain that her parents had meals and dutifully sat through every news show about the accident that they insisted upon watching since Brett's funeral.

So adept had she become at hiding her own feelings that she hadn't even known she was headed for a breakdown. When she'd passed out in school with no memory of what had happened, her parents finally took action. She'd been hospitalized for a week and returned home only when the psychiatrist assigned to her case had been satisfied that she would be given the proper care.

It had been then that her grandmother had stepped in and brought Paige to live with her for the summer. From that time on, Paige had done everything she could to bury the day Brett had died. She read no accounts of the accident, watched no more news reports rehashing it and, when the anniversary of it occurred, studiously avoided all media. Though her brother lived on in her heart, she had effectively blocked out the day he'd died.

Aware that she'd remained locked in the past for too long, she looked up to find Liam watching her, eyes dark with concern. "You're remembering, too, aren't you?" He stroked her jawline with his thumb, the gesture tender.

She didn't have words and could only nod. With an act of will, she dragged herself back to the present and focused on Liam. He was still hurting after Mrs. Hawkins's attack, and who could blame him? He'd saved the woman's husband and all she could do was berate him.

"You did the best you could. More than anyone could expect." Paige winced at the banality of the words. They sounded lame even to her own ears.

Liam slammed down his knife with enough force to have other diners turn and stare. "It wasn't enough."

A waiter looked up and started in Liam's direction until he waved him away. "Sorry."

"No problem."

"Is there anything else on the trip home that stands out?" she asked. "Anything at all?"

Paige wasn't going to be able to talk him out of his guilt, so he was grateful that she turned the subject back to what had happened on the bus ride itself. Something was there, if they could only identify it. His gut churned as he reviewed the bus ride in his mind.

A beat passed, then another, as he gathered his thoughts.

"Just the normal ragging on each other. We were a bunch of kids, high on life, on winning the last game of the season. You know how kids are. We thought we were invincible, that nothing bad could touch us." He snorted out a laugh at the irony of it. "We couldn't have been more wrong."

"What about the trip to the game? Did anything out of the ordinary happen then? Something that when you looked back it gave you pause?"

"I wish I could say there was. The cheerleaders led us in some cheers. I remember Marie telling me that she'd have a special cheer just for me at the game. And she did." The memory had a smile slipping onto his lips. "She was the prettiest thing I'd ever seen, standing at the top of the pyramid, her blond hair blowing in the wind.

"Only the thing with Sam sticks out." Liam hunched his shoulders in a defeated gesture. "And I'm not even sure if there was really something there or if I imagined it. I don't want to waste our time on something that might not even be real."

"Memories can be tricky, especially after all this time, but you're an observant guy. If you say there was something there, I believe you."

He flashed a smile. "Thanks." His smile vanished as quickly as it had appeared. "Even if there were, what would it matter? Sam died before the killings started. He can't have anything to do with what's going on now. Not that he would. Sam never hurt anyone. It wasn't in him. He was the kindest, gentlest man I've ever known."

"I don't know that it does matter," Paige said. "I'm reaching, trying to come up with something that would explain why these accidents/murders started when they did. You said they started about six weeks ago. When did you say Sam died?"

With her memory, she already knew the answer, but he understood that she wanted him to make the connection.

"Six weeks ago," he said. "But that doesn't mean anything. It can't."

"The timeline fits," she pointed out.

"Coincidence?"

She raised a brow. "I don't put much stock in coincidences."

"Neither do I," Liam admitted. "I still don't see how Sam could be connected to what's happening, but I can't deny the timing."

"I think we need to take a closer look at Sam Newley, see if we can find something that connects him with the killings. Something happened to him that day, something that turned him—how did you put it?—'real still.' I have a feeling it could be important."

"Important how?"

"That's what we need to find out."

Like Paige, Liam didn't believe in coincidences. In fact, a healthy skepticism of them had saved his life more than once when he was deployed. One incident in particular stood out.

A local shopkeeper, one who had refused to help the Americans in the past, had suddenly experienced a change of heart. He sought out Liam and told him that a certain warlord would be at the marketplace in two days' time. It just so happened that Liam's unit had been searching for the man for months.

Liam and his unit had shown up, but not at the time the shopkeeper named. Instead, they arrived early to see him deep in conversation with a known associate of the warlord. It had been a setup from the first. They'd taken the associate as well as the merchant prisoner and had leveraged them for information.

If Liam had allowed himself to believe in such a beneficial coincidence, he and his team would have been wiped out.

So when Paige suggested a visit to Sam's brother, Liam was on board.

They drove to Sam's family home. Sam had bought the house from his parents as an investment and had invited his younger brother to live with him. It was a brick ranch, solidly in the middle class, with a well-kept yard fronting it and neat flower beds flanking it on either side.

Jerry Newley opened the door, gave a surprised look, then welcomed them inside. He was of medium height, with dark hair that failed to disguise a slightly receding hairline.

"Liam McKenzie. I didn't expect to see you here."

Liam made the introductions.

Jerry shook Paige's hand. "Ms. Walker, glad to meet you." He turned his attention back to Liam. "I've been meaning to call you and say how much I appreciated you coming to Sam's funeral and for the flower arrangement," Jerry said. "He always liked you."

Liam flushed at the thanks he didn't deserve. "I should have visited more often. I didn't realize how bad things had gotten with Sam. The last I'd heard, he was in remission."

"Sam didn't want his friends to know that the cancer had come back. If you remember, he was always kind of private, didn't want any attention."

"I remember. Still, I should have come to see him more. We shared something important."

"The accident." Jerry's voice went flat. "It changed everything, didn't it? I was too young to remember much about it, but I knew that Sam changed after it. He closed in on himself for a while, like he didn't want anything or anyone to touch him. I always thought that's why he went into research."

When he paused, as though overcome with emotion, Liam glanced around the room. It hadn't changed much since the years he and Sam had been friends. Family pictures topped a mantel, including one of a school class. From the year stamped on it, it had to have been Jerry's class.

Something nudged Liam's memory, something that could be important. The more he tried to recall it, though, the more it eluded him.

Jerry talked nonstop. Not at all like his tall older brother, who had given new meaning to the word *quiet*. Jerry kept up a constant stream of chatter that Liam did his best to sift through for any nuggets he and Paige could use.

Liam let a nod answer for him during Jerry's recollections. He didn't want to color any impressions Jerry might have gleaned from Sam with his own memories.

"You might have heard of the accidents that killed three of the survivors in the last six weeks."

Jerry's nod was a quick jerk of the head. "I have. In a way, I'm glad Sam is gone, that he didn't have to see that. He said there was a bond between the survivors that could never be broken."

Liam worked to contain his excitement that Jerry had brought up Sam's memories himself. "I wondered if Sam might have said something else to you about the bus accident." He kept his voice casual, not wanting to let on how much he was hoping for answers from Jerry.

Jerry angled his head, slanting Liam a curious look. "Like what?"

"Nothing in particular. Maybe he remembered something, something he shared with only you. After all, you were brothers."

"Sam never talked about it much. He told me flat out that he didn't want to remember what happened that day." Jerry gave a slight smile. "Except for you and what you did. He said you kept going back in the water until...well, until there wasn't anything more you could do. He always looked up to you. Did you know that?"

"I remember it being the other way around with me looking up to him." Liam shifted subjects. "Did Sam ever say much about that day?"

Jerry shook his head. "About the only thing he said was that you were the hero of the day."

"That's not how some see it," Liam said.

"What do you mean?"

"They blame me for not saving everyone." As if it were yesterday, memories bombarded him.

Jerry looked surprised. "Sam said you kept going back down, even when you were so tired that you could barely lift your arms."

He shrugged. "It's over and doesn't matter anymore."

"It matters to someone," Paige said and explained what was going on.

The younger man's eyes widened. "You mean someone's killing survivors from that day?"

"That's what it looks like," Liam said.

"No kidding. Then I really am glad Sam's not here to see it," Jerry repeated. "He wasn't one to think bad about anyone. It wasn't in him. He was always willing to give a person a second try."

"You're right. Even at seventeen, Sam had his head on straight," Liam said. "Did he ever say anything, anything at all? You said he didn't want to remember that day. Did he mention anything in particular he wanted to forget?"

"You mean beyond the obvious? That five kids died?"

Jerry's voice had an edge now, with a bite of sarcasm that Liam chose to ignore. From the expression on Paige's face, she had noted it, as well.

"Sorry," Jerry said. "Didn't mean to snap at you that way. It's just that talking about Sam brings up memories. Most of them good, but not all. He pulled away from me after the accident and never really came back."

"No problem," Liam said easily. "Most of us don't want to remember what happened that day, but it sticks with us anyway. I figured it might have been the same with Sam."

"Sometimes Sam would get a far-off look in his eyes, like he was thinking about something that he'd rather not be thinking about. When that happened, I knew he was reliving the day of the accident. It changed him."

"It changed all of us," Liam said.

"Like I said, Sam was pretty closemouthed." Jerry poked his tongue in the corner of his cheek. "You know Sam. He never said much even if he was feeling chatty." Jerry's mouth curved into a half smile.

Liam smiled in response. "*Chatty*'s not a word I'd use to describe Sam."

"I wish I could help you out. Sam and I were never close until this last year, when he got sick and I moved in to take care of him." He shook his head regretfully. "That's on me. I should have made more of an effort."

The words were right. Why didn't Liam believe them? He dismissed that.

Paige stood, pulled out a card from her pocket and pressed it into Jerry's hand. "If you think of something, please let us know. We're trying to put a stop to this before anyone else is hurt."

Jerry closed his hand around the card. "You can count on it."

Liam stuck out his hand. "Thanks for your time. We appreciate you seeing us."

"I'm just sorry I couldn't be of more help. Though I wasn't on the bus that day, I always felt close to the survivors because of Sam."

"You never know what will help," Liam said.

Liam and Paige took their leave and returned to the car.

"That didn't get us much," he said. "But it was good to talk about Sam. He was one of a kind."

"I wish I'd known him."

"You would have liked him. He wasn't one of the popular kids, but he stood out. Maybe because of that. You could always count on him to do the right thing."

At S&J's office, they looked at the case from various perspectives, but none brought them closer to an answer.

A huge yawn caught Liam unaware, and he rubbed at eyes, gritty with fatigue. He was so exhausted he could barely put one thought after another.

"Maybe we'll see things from a different angle tomorrow," Paige said.

"Maybe." But at that moment, his mind wasn't on angles. It was on the courage Paige showed at every danger they faced. It was on the steadfastness of her belief. It was on the woman herself who refused to give up no matter what was thrown at them.

He yanked his thoughts away from Paige. She was helping him because it was her job. Nothing more. He should have felt better at the self-directed reminder.

But he didn't.

SEVEN

Morning came in a blast of cold and rain. After being deployed in Afghanistan, Liam didn't let a bit of cold bother him. Temperatures in the mountains there often plummeted below freezing. Though the days were blistering hot, nighttime brought on a bone-deep cold that was all the more bitter due to the need to remain absolutely motionless while on watch.

When Paige suggested visiting Reva Thomas, the sister of Liam's old girlfriend, he agreed.

Even with the rain, the countryside was dazzling, the green fields lush and full of crops, the occasional barn painted brick-red.

When a shot punctured a tire, Liam steered the car to the side of the road, then motioned for Paige to climb out the passenger side. He drew his weapon and quickly followed.

He scanned the fields but didn't spot the shooter. A trained sniper could be anywhere. Another shot landed terrifyingly close to where Paige was crouched behind the car. She, too, had her weapon drawn.

"I going to make a wide circle, see if I can spot the shooter," he said.

"You're the client," she pointed out. "I'm the one who's supposed to protect you."

"Okay. We go together."

They belly-crawled through the thick rows of soybeans in the general direction from which the bullets came.

When Liam spotted a glint of metal, he gestured to Paige. "If I can get behind him, I can take him out."

She used her thumb to point to her chest. "My job."

He was about to argue when a third shot landed not far from their heads.

Liam had a pretty good idea where the sniper was positioned now. Though Paige had excellent skills, it was Liam who had military training. He should be the one to go after the shooter.

"Stay here and cover me." He didn't give her time to object but took off in that direction and came within yards of the man. With close-cropped hair and a muscular build, he looked ex-military or ex–law enforcement or both.

Liam must have somehow alerted his prey, for his adversary turned and lifted his head, as though scenting the air. When he spotted Liam, he fired, but Liam was too quick, diving for cover in an irrigation ditch and returning fire.

The slam of a door and roar of an engine were brash in the morning quiet. Liam's quarry had escaped.

He returned to where he'd left Paige. "Missed him."

"That wasn't some peashooter he was firing," she said.

"No. Unless I'm way off, it was a 125 Sniper Vortex." The Vortex was a particularly lethal weapon, a favorite among serious shooters. He'd seen it in action when he'd been deployed and knew just how deadly it was.

Fortunately, the trunk had a spare and Liam set about changing the tire. They stopped at the first gas station they found and had the punctured tire repaired and placed back on the vehicle.

Nearly an hour later, they were once more on their way to Reva Thomas's place.

"Tell me about Reva," Paige said.

"She was my girlfriend's little sister. I was too wrapped up in Marie to pay her much attention."

"You and Marie were the perfect couple in high school, you the football star and she the head cheerleader."

"I don't know that we were perfect, but I cared for her." He'd cared a lot and had thought his life was over when she'd died. Knowing that he had no choice but to go on, he'd finished out the school year and graduated, but without any of the satisfaction he would have felt at one time.

Looking back, he realized that his feelings for Marie had been those of a callow boy and would have no doubt faded in time. She'd been his first love and, therefore, special, but they hadn't had the foundation of real love to sustain them.

They'd been in love with the idea of being in love, not the genuine thing, and, though he hated to admit it, the same had been true of his marriage. He and Joelle had thought they were in love, when, in reality, all they'd had was an attraction that all but disappeared within the first year. Jonah was the one good thing to come from their union.

"Losing her must have been rough." Immediately, Paige stopped herself. "I'm sorry. That was a stupid thing to say."

"Marie and I talked about the future, even about going to college together. When she died, I thought I'd lost part of myself, but life went on."

"Did you keep in touch with her family?"

"For a while. Reva was on the bus that day along with Marie. She was equipment manager for the cheerleaders."

"Was she one of the kids you pulled out?"

"No. She made it out on her own."

"I read she's now mayor of Willow Springs."

Liam pulled up memories of his onetime girlfriend's little sister. "She was smart and pretty, but she got on Marie's nerves. She always wanted to hang out with us."

Paige gave a wry smile. "The plight of the little sister. I was the same way with Brett."

Liam navigated his way through morning traffic and pulled up in front of the house where he'd spent so many afternoons.

The Thomas home looked well maintained and even sported a new roofline with the addition of a second story and gabled windows. Though it wasn't overly large, it had an air of prosperity, as did the neighborhood itself.

"Reva's done well for herself," Liam murmured as he knocked.

The door opened, and recognition lit Reva's features as she smiled. "Liam McKenzie. It's been too long. Well, except for seeing you at the funerals of our friends in the last six weeks, and that doesn't count." She hugged him, then stood back and gave him a once-over. "I heard you'd joined the army, made Delta. It looks good on you. Really good."

"Thanks. I've been back for a while now." He made the introductions. "Reva Thomas. Paige Walker."

Reva glanced at Paige. "I remember you. Smart girl. Skipped a couple of grades, right?"

"Right. We graduated in the same class."

"That's right." Reva turned her attention back to Liam. "How's it been going?"

He didn't answer directly. "Can we come in?"

"Of course. Where are my manners? It's been a hectic morning. City business, you know. I was able to work from home this morning, which is a blessing, given how frantic my life's become."

"I heard you were mayor of Willow Springs. Congratulations."

"Thanks." She preened a bit.

Liam didn't begrudge her the success she'd found. Even as a teenager, Reva always had her eye fixed on bigger and better things.

He gestured around. "You've done well for yourself."

Another preen. "When my parents moved to Miami, I bought the place from them and did some fixing up. Can I offer you anything? Sweet tea? Coffee?"

"No, thanks," Paige said.

"Now that we've gotten the small talk out of the way, tell me what's brought you here."

"We're here to find out what you remember from the day of the accident."

Bringing her hands to her lips, Reva made a sound of distress. "I've tried to forget that day."

"I get it," Liam said. "I feel the same way, but some things have happened that have us wanting to revisit it."

"Oh?"

"You mentioned seeing me at the funerals of our friends. You knew that they had all recently died in accidents?" He made a question out of it.

"What does that have to do with you paying me a visit?"

"We're not sure that they were accidents," Liam said, choosing his words with care.

"What do you mean?"

"We think those deaths were disguised to look like accidents. They were all survivors of the bus accident. We're checking with families of the kids who died that day to see if there might be a connection. Since you're a survivor, too, I wanted to give you a head's up and to ask you to let me know if you notice anything odd, anything that makes you uneasy."

"I appreciate the warning." She gave a delicate shiver, then eyed him shrewdly. "There's more, isn't there? You're thinking that one of us might be behind what's going on."

"You're very quick, Ms. Thomas," Paige said.

"It's Reva." Out came a flash of whiter-than-white teeth in a patented politician's smile. "I'm smart enough to do the math." She turned to Liam. "But I have a hard time seeing members of our friends' families going around killing people."

"Maybe you won't have such a hard time when I tell you that some people still carry grudges," he said and explained about Mr. Howard and Pope's wife and son. "Now someone is trying to kill me."

"I can't believe it," Reva said, shaking her head. "I never bore you or any of the other kids who survived ill will. After all, I'm a survivor, too."

Liam recalled that she'd taken some teasing over her job as equipment manager, as it didn't carry the prestige of being on the cheerleading squad itself. Somehow she'd managed to get out of the bus on her own and swim to the surface.

Because she was younger than the other survivors, she had been largely lost in the shuffle and no one had paid much attention to her. When she was remembered, it was always as "Marie's little sister."

"I know. You were one of the few people who was still speaking to me by the end of school."

"It wasn't your fault that kids died any more than it was mine. I'm sorry, Liam. I remember most of the folks treated you like a hero, but I guess some blamed you for not getting their kids out. You did your best. That's what I told my parents when they were grieving Marie, the same as I told everyone else."

"Thanks, Reva. That means a lot."

"About these accidents…" she spread her hands "… I just don't know. I didn't realize that they were anything but that until you showed up. Now I'm wondering if I'm at risk." A delicate shudder punctuated her words as twin lines worked their way across her brow.

"Have you noticed anyone following you?" Paige asked.

"No. But I've been pretty preoccupied." Her worried look relaxed into a thoughtful expression. "I can ask my staffers if they've noticed anyone strange hanging around. They're pretty protective of me." She gave a light laugh. "We've become a kind of family. They believe in me and what I want for the town, for the state."

"Family is good, wherever it comes from," Liam said.

"That's what I thought. My staff is the best. They make sure I remember to eat and sleep. I'm fortunate to have them. All in all, I'm doing okay."

"I'd say you've done more than okay," Paige said. "You're very young to be mayor, and now you're running for the state senate."

"Thanks. It's a lot to take on. I hope I'm up to the job." The words were modest, but the smug tilt of her smile was not. Its brilliance radiated a confidence that said she was not only up to the job but would soon move on to even bigger things.

"I'm sure you are," Liam said.

"I really wish I could help. After I graduated, I didn't keep in touch with kids from school much. It was—" she lifted a slim shoulder "—too hard with losing Marie. And I was never really a part of the rest of you. I know what the kids thought, that I was just a hanger-on, being cheerleading equipment manager. It wasn't much, but it let me hang out with all you handsome football players." She gave Liam a wink and reached for his hand, held it a beat too long. "Marie always said you were a hero. You proved it that day."

Uncomfortable with the praise, Liam ducked his head. "Thanks," he mumbled. "But I wasn't a hero any more than anyone else."

"You were a hero in my book. What you did took guts."

"Thanks, Reva. Like I said, not everyone feels that way."

"You know what I do when people don't like me? I put them out of my mind and move on." She snapped her fingers. "Easy-peasy."

After a few more minutes, Liam and Paige made their goodbyes. Back in the truck, he turned to her. "What did you think?"

"She comes across as straightforward."

"'Comes across'? Does that mean you don't think she is?"

"It means I don't know. She's ambitious and is aiming for bigger things. Things that will take her beyond Willow Springs, even beyond the state capital."

Liam was dubious. "Being mayor of Willow Springs and running for state senator doesn't exactly make her a power player."

"But that isn't where she intends to end up."

"How do you know?"

"Her shoes."

He shot her an incredulous look. "Her shoes?"

"Jimmy Choo. Trust me. I know good shoes even

though I can't afford them. She's dressing for the job she wants. I'm guessing Congress. From there it's a hop, skip and jump to governor. And from there, who knows?" Paige sent him a teasing smile. "She had a crush on you back in the day. Like most of the girls."

"You, too?" Why had he asked that? It came off as sounding desperate.

But Paige didn't seem to mind answering. "Of course. I had the biggest crush of all on you. I was afraid to even look at you for fear you'd discover my secret."

And now? But this time he had the sense to keep his mouth shut. And what was he doing, quizzing Paige about feelings that were fifteen years old?

"You were big-man-on-campus," she said, appearing not to notice his silence. "Every boy wanted to be you and every girl wanted to date you."

He shook his head, partly in negation of the boy he had been. "I was young and full of myself. My head was so big that I'm surprised I could get my football helmet on." He sent her a curious look. "I'm flattered a girl like you ever paid attention to me. You were always studying."

"I was trying to get through high school as quickly as possible. Those years weren't happy ones for me."

"I'm sorry. Sorry I didn't see how lonely you were. I was Brett's friend. I should have noticed, should have paid attention."

"You have nothing to feel sorry about. All the girls were dying to be asked out by you. But you had eyes only for Marie."

He remembered. Marie had been everything to him. Looking back, he wondered whether they would have remained together after graduation. She had always dreamed of going to New York and starring on Broadway. As for him…he hadn't looked beyond the next football game. *Shallow* didn't begin to describe him.

Until the accident.

Until everything had changed.

As Liam drove, Paige looked out the window at the woods, her gaze taking in towering pines and dense underbrush as she stored away impressions of Reva Thomas. The woman was pretty, smart and clearly ambitious. Her attitude regarding people who didn't like her seemed a healthy one, if a bit shallow. Better that than internalizing everything as she did, Paige reflected.

Her thoughts moved on to Jerry Newley. Something about yesterday's visit bothered her, but she couldn't identify it. Jerry had been welcoming enough, so it wasn't that. Something she'd seen in the house, maybe, but the memory wouldn't jog loose. She was left with a niggling sense of having missed something important, leaving her feeling unsettled. Grasping at it, she thought she had it until it spun and floated away. From experience, she knew that the harder she thought on it, the more elusive it became.

"Where to now?" Liam asked.

"I want to head back to S&J to do some research about people's finances. Whoever is behind this has access to money. It isn't cheap to stage accidents or hire trained men."

"Good plan."

But just as he said it, two high-riding pickups drove up on their tail. Liam slowed to let them pass. One did, while the other remained behind.

"Our shooter is back," Liam said, "and he's brought a friend."

Within minutes, the trucks had sandwiched Liam's

rented car between them. Hemmed in, Liam and Paige had nowhere to go.

Paige assessed their options, a steely coldness overtaking her. Escape first. Fight later. Only they weren't given the choice as the pickups closed the space.

"Can you take out the truck behind us?" Liam asked.

"Watch me."

She rolled down her window and aimed at the front end of the truck following them, putting three shots in the engine block, a much easier target than a tire. Taking out a tire on a moving vehicle wasn't nearly as easy as television cop shows portrayed.

That took care of the men behind them, but she and Liam still had to deal with the truck just ahead of them.

It sped up, then did a quick 180 in the road, barreling straight at them.

"Hang on," Liam said as he swerved to miss the huge black truck.

She was doing just that.

He overcompensated, and the car spun off the road. "We're going over."

Instinctively, she braced herself.

The car teetered on the edge of the road, then rolled down an embankment.

The impact was fierce. Metal crunched. Glass shattered. Airbags deployed.

Two men from the second truck were heading toward Paige and Liam's disabled vehicle.

"We've got to get out of here," she said.

Paige and Liam scrambled from the vehicle and plunged into the marsh just seconds before the men reached them.

The wind made a mournful noise, tickling the back of her neck before it slid down her shirt in a chilly blast.

She shivered and wondered how long she and Liam had before the rain started and things turned really hairy.

She didn't have to wait long.

The rain came in stinging pellets, unbelievably cold.

With their pursuers gaining with every second, Paige and Liam ran through the marsh, Liam taking the lead. Something about the spongy ground just ahead of them sent off warning bells in her brain.

"Wait," she yelled. "Quicksand!"

EIGHT

Her cry came too late. Liam was already waist-deep in the deadly bog.

She had to get him out before he sank any deeper. She undid her shirt, grateful she had a long-sleeved T-shirt underneath. After knotting the end of one sleeve and wrapping the other around her hand, she tossed it toward Liam.

"It's not long enough."

All the while, the men were getting closer, ever closer.

"Get out of here," Liam ordered. "It's me they want. Not you. You can still save yourself."

As that didn't deserve an answer, she didn't give one. She needed something to lengthen the reach of her shirt. Looking around, she saw a long branch. That should do it.

A closer look showed that the wood was rotting. It would crumble to pieces before she could pull Liam from the quicksand. She poked beneath it and saw a thick vine. If she tied her shirt to one end, the length should do.

Rain and wind obscured much of her vision so that she could barely make out Liam. When she saw him, he was trying to push his way through the quicksand.

"Stop thrashing around," she yelled. "You'll only make it worse."

Voices of the men chasing them reached her. She had to get Liam out now.

Hurry.

Fingers fumbling with cold and fear, she struggled to tie the shirt to the vine. At last she had what she hoped was a reasonably strong knot.

She whipped the vine into the air much as a fly fisherman would cast his rod. Her first try didn't land anywhere near Liam, and she tried again.

There.

"Got it," he shouted and grabbed hold of the shirtsleeve.

"Just hold on while I pull. Don't try to help."

For a man like Liam, accustomed to taking action, to saving others rather than the other way around, that would likely grate, but there was no choice.

Pulling Liam through the quicksand was like pulling a canoe through molasses. They weren't moving fast enough, not with the voices of their pursuers growing closer with every minute.

She redoubled her efforts, calling on the Lord's help. *I know I can't do this on my own, Lord. I also know that with Your help, we can save Liam. Please give me the strength I need.*

"It's no use," Liam shouted, his words carried on the wind. "Get out of here."

"Not going to happen."

Her arms felt rubbery, her shoulders bunched into tight knots, but she didn't let up. Couldn't. Just when she was certain she couldn't pull anymore, a fresh burst of strength surged through her and she tugged with all her might.

"We're doing it," she yelled over the wind. "We're doing it. Don't try to help, just hold on."

Another foot gained. And another. She doubled down on her efforts and put her whole self into the task.

Just when she thought they were home free, a shot rang out, dangerously close to where she stood. Their pursuers had found them, but she couldn't let up on her task. Not now.

A second shot quickly followed. Then a third. Or at least she thought it was a shot. With the wind whipping the air with all its might and the rain pelting, it was hard to tell. How many shots had she heard? Three? Four? Five?

And how many men were there? The men who had run them off the road could have called for backup.

Don't think about that. Liam needed her focus. She kept pulling.

The Lord was in charge, she reminded herself. He would protect her and Liam if her faith didn't waver. She recalled one of her favorite scriptures from 2 Kings. *Fear not: for they that be with us are more than they that be with them.*

"Get out of here, Paige."

She ignored the order just as she had the others. Her hands were raw from the scrape of the vine against her palms. Even through the rain, she could see the blood running down her wrist and arm, but she refused to let go. The blood turned her hands slippery, but she dared not take a second to wipe them on her pants.

Liam's life depended upon her. She knew the Lord was doing His part, and she just needed to do hers. He didn't ask that she do more than that of which she was capable, only that she do her best.

I'm trying, Lord. I'm trying.

Another shot. *Ignore it.* The shooter couldn't see any

more than she could. He was firing blindly. The thought brought little comfort, though.

Three more yards. That was all they needed. Only three more yards. *You can do it.* The words chanted in her mind, and she matched her rhythm to their beat. Hand over hand, she kept up the punishing pace.

"We're almost there." She panted out the words with each pull on the vine.

Liam was moving closer, so close she could almost touch him. She longed to do away with the vine-shirt contraption and pull him the rest of the way herself, but she dared not give way to the temptation. If his greater weight pulled her into the quicksand, they'd both be lost.

After another superhuman effort on her part, he stumbled to safety. When another bullet whizzed heart-stoppingly close to them, he pushed her down and covered her with his own body. Mud filled her nostrils and mouth, and she did her best to spit it out.

The rain and wind that she'd decried only moments ago now served to shield them from their enemies. So did the quicksand. Without knowing how far the pool of deadly mud reached, the men couldn't risk coming any closer.

A blessing in disguise. Grateful as she was for it, she'd been hoping for a blessing that wasn't covered in mud and muck.

Liam held Paige to the ground. The shots continued to go wild. That told him the shooters weren't first-tier operators. Even poor shots, though, could find their target occasionally, if only by accident.

"We can't see them in this stuff," one of the men said, voice carrying on the wind. "Let's get out of here. Maybe the swamp will do our work for us. There are wild boar out here, not to mention bears."

"I'm with you."

The men retreated.

Still, Paige and Liam didn't move. It could be a trick. Terrorists in Afghanistan had been fond of pretending to leave an area, only to rise up from the sand and pick off unwary soldiers who'd believed the enemy had departed.

When long moments had elapsed, Liam got to his feet and offered Paige his hand.

Cautiously, she stood. "That was close."

"Too close." He heaved out a breath. Another. "Thanks. You saved my life."

"All in a day's work. Besides, I owed you." Her words were strained, as though she had trouble squeezing them out. At the same time, an unmistakable electric current crackled in the air.

He dipped his head and came within an inch of touching his lips to hers. He didn't want to dwell on the warmth of her voice or the lips that were but a scant inch from his own.

The moment passed. His hoarse laugh relieved the rest of the tension. "I'm covered with mud and stink of the swamp."

"And I'm not much better."

He focused on picking his way through the slippery floor of the swamp, careful not to trip on the vines that stretched across the ground.

They made their way out of the swamp, all the while listening for any sounds that hinted they weren't alone, that the men who had attacked them were lying in wait. The last thing they needed was to let down their guard and invite another attack. Though the men weren't professionals, they could still be deadly.

The sounds of animals rustling in the underbrush gave credence to the men's comments about wild boar and bear. Pumas also prowled the swamp, along with snakes of all kinds. Any could easily kill a person.

At last, they made it to the car.

"It's not going anywhere," Liam announced unnecessarily.

"Then we're in for a hike."

During the long trek to find cell coverage, Paige examined what had almost happened between herself and Liam. Granted, emotions were running high. They'd nearly been killed by their pursuers, and he could have died in the quagmire of quicksand.

The almost-kiss was the result of an adrenaline surge, relief that they were still alive. That was all. Nothing more, she assured herself and did her best to ignore the whisper of anticipation that still shivered through her. Then why was she having such a hard time convincing herself of it?

The recent rain had turned the ground slick. When her foot slid, Liam steadied her with a hand to her elbow.

"Careful."

She also needed to be careful when it came to her feelings for her client. She could take a wrong step and slide down a slippery path from which there was no coming back.

Think about something else. "Tell me about your time in Afghanistan," she said. "You said you'd seen too much to ever believe in the Lord's goodness again."

He was silent so long that she feared he wasn't going to answer. When he spoke, his voice was so low that she had to strain to hear it.

"The Stand was one of those places where war had

sucked the life out of the land and the people. For the most part, the people were good and hardworking, trying to make a living in a harsh land and impossible circumstances. Some of them even helped the US military, and we came to depend upon them.

"A young boy, about fifteen, ran errands for us. He knew the ins and outs of Jalalabad and fed us information whenever he could. I warned him not to take risks, but he wanted to help us rid the land of the terrorists. He told me once that that was the best way he knew to help his family and his people.

"He managed to infiltrate a terrorist group and gave us valuable intel. But he was discovered as a spy. What they did to him…" Liam shook his head. "He died a horrible death because he was trying to help us. I might as well have put a bullet in him myself."

"I'm so sorry, but you must know that that wasn't your fault."

"You don't know all of it."

"Tell me the rest."

"I ordered men into battles I knew we couldn't win. And because of that, good men died. Men who had wives and children and sweethearts and parents at home. Men who just wanted to serve their country. Men who deserved better.

"Does your Lord love a man who did that and who walked away without a scratch when his men were left bleeding and broken and worse? Does He love a man who is so messed up that he flinches when he hears carts at the supermarket bang together? Or who can't take his son to a Fourth of July party because the explosions make him think he's still at war?" His voice gained strength and volume with every question. "Does your Lord love that man? If He does, why does He let war happen in the first place? If He is all powerful and good, why doesn't He stop it?"

The words were so strangled that she could barely make out the last ones. Her heart ached for him, for a soul so damaged and ravaged by the ugliness of war. She longed to reach for him, to hold him against her and promise that the Lord could help heal the scars in his heart, but she kept her arms at her sides and her words locked inside, knowing that Liam wasn't ready to hear them.

"I'm sorry." The inadequacy of her words mocked what he had just shared, but they were all she had.

"I don't want your pity."

"And you're not getting it," she returned. "Sorrow isn't the same as pity. A man as smart as you should know that."

He flushed. "Now I'm the one who's sorry."

Paige understood grief. More than most, probably. Her brother and then her fiancé had both died far too early, but telling Liam that he wasn't alone wasn't the way to comfort him.

Grief couldn't be willed away. Neither could it be ordered to cease. Grief lived on because people needed that connection to those who had been lost. Liam had cared for the young boy who had sacrificed his life for his people. He'd also cared for the men in his command.

He probably wouldn't put his feelings in those words.

She regarded Liam with his dirty hair, mud-encrusted clothes and tortured eyes. When they found the killer—and they would—would he forgive himself for the death of the boy and those of his men? And as she helped him, would she be able to forgive herself for not being able to save Ethan?

In putting an end to the killings, would either of them

find the peace they sought? Or were they both chasing the impossible?

She wanted to ask him everything, and so she asked him nothing.

NINE

When a beat-up truck stopped and the driver offered them a ride, Liam and Paige accepted eagerly.

"Thanks," Liam told the driver, a farmer with a hat as beat-up as his truck and a craggy face that spoke of long hours in the Georgia sun.

"No problem. I figure if you don't mind riding with springs poking you in the backside, I don't mind a little dirt." He eyed them curiously. "Something tells me there's a story there behind all that dried mud. If you don't mind my saying so, you both stink of the swamp."

"You're right, there's a story," Liam said, "but you don't have time to hear it. Where is it convenient to drop us?"

The driver named an address close to S&J headquarters.

"Great," Paige said. "And thank you."

He let them out and they hoofed it the rest of the way to S&J. Inside, Paige directed Liam to a men's room.

"There're some men's clothes here that we keep just for these occasions. I'll bring them to you."

"Thanks."

He found a spacious bathroom, complete with shower.

A half hour later, he met her in her office. "I thought I'd never get the mud off me. Or the stink."

"Same here. There's something about the swamp smell that sticks to you." She sniffed. "I'm going to be smelling like it for the next week."

Liam arranged for another rental car to be delivered to the S&J office. "My insurance agent is going to hit the roof. This is the second claim I've made in a week."

"It's a good thing you got total coverage," Paige said, sharing a smile with him. Then her smile faded. "I still say what's happening goes back to the day of the accident. There's something there, something that would make sense of everything if we could only identify it."

"I've racked my brain trying to come up with something. Anything. Nothing stands out, except for what I told you about Sam, and I'm not even sure that that's real."

"Describe Sam on the way home. You said he got real still, but did he say anything?"

"I tried talking with him, and he said he was trying to figure something out. Then he leaned back against the seat, closed his eyes. He didn't say anything else. I waited to see if he wanted to talk, hung around, just *there*. But he didn't open his eyes. After a while, I backed off and left him alone. The rest of the guys were celebrating, telling stories about how great we'd played, making plans for how we'd party when we got back. The best I know, I was the last person he talked to before the accident."

"That's all?"

"All that I can remember."

Why did the thing with Sam stick out? It was a throw-away incident, yet it stuck in Liam's mind with surprising tenacity.

Was it because he didn't want to remember how he'd left his friends behind? Was it because he could still hear Danny's and Brett's voices in his mind urging him to go ahead? Was it because he couldn't bear knowing that he had left five friends to die?

Paige understood that Liam was caught up in the past. She didn't want to disturb him, but spending too much time thinking of what might have been didn't do anyone any good. Nor did beating yourself up for what couldn't be changed.

She ought to know.

After Ethan's death, she'd blamed herself and had refused to listen to calmer voices, all saying that no one could have foreseen what had happened.

Blood rushed to her ears as she was suddenly plunged into the past. Memories, harsh snapshots in black and white, hit her with such force that if she'd been standing, her knees would have buckled.

As it was, she gripped the edge of her desk, trying to hold on to the here and now, but the past reached out and grabbed hold of her. In an effort to keep from crying out, she bit her lower lip, the physical pain helping to ebb her panic.

It had been a routine operation, one that should have gone off smoothly. She and Ethan were undercover, posing as a couple looking to buy arms to sell overseas. Expensive clothes, designer bag and flashy jewelry had sold the look while a briefcase full of cash had cemented their introduction to one of the top arms dealers on the East Coast.

They'd met their mark in an abandoned factory where shadows cast by a harsh overhead light vied with the dank darkness that permeated the corners of the huge room. Well aware that the boss's men were no doubt hidden in the corners had her subtly checking them out, trying to identify the location of the tangos.

Everything was going by the book right up until the meeting with the big man. He rarely came out of hiding to conduct business, but they'd made the deal too sweet to pass up and had insisted upon doing business with the head of the organization.

But the boss's second in command had taken one look at Ethan and drawn his gun. "He's a fed."

A sting operation that Ethan had spearheaded eight years ago had rounded up a dozen or more foot soldiers, one of whom was now the boss's right-hand man. For keeping his mouth shut upon his arrest, he'd been rewarded with a high-level position in the organization.

Instantly weapons were drawn, and though Ethan and Paige had tried to brazen their way out, they knew they were in trouble. Fortunately, she'd had a mini-transistor hidden in the ostentatious jewel pinned to the lapel of her $3,000 suit.

Backup arrived and, for a few moments, she'd thought she and Ethan were home free, but the henchman who had identified him had wanted revenge and, at the last minute, had shot him.

As soon as Paige had seen the dark blood—death blood—gushing from the gut wound, she knew it was too late. Still, she did her best to stanch the flow, yelling for paramedics, praying with all her might.

Ethan had been given a hero's funeral and she had packed up her bags and moved from the home she'd planned to share with him.

"Guilt is an equal-opportunity taskmaster," she said now. "It exacts a price from anyone trapped in its snare."

"Want to tell me about it?"

Paige told Liam about Ethan, recalling her earlier thoughts. She continued, "Everything should have been all right, even at the end when Ethan was pegged as a fed. Our backup arrived and I turned my back, just for a minute, to talk to the supervisory agent. I thought the man was out of commission—I shot him myself—but he had enough hate in him to make sure he took Ethan down with him."

"If I'd had my partner's back, maybe he'd still be here."

"*If* is a dangerous word," Liam remarked. "I've used it myself. *If* I'd been faster. *If* I'd been stronger. The world's ifs will destroy us if we let them."

"I'm sorry. I've made this about me. I didn't mean to do that."

He reached for her hand, squeezed it once. Twice. "I'm glad you did."

So was she. To her surprise, she didn't pull away.

"Thank you for telling me that," Liam said. "It couldn't have been easy."

"It's me who should thank you for listening. You have enough on your mind without my adding to it."

"I needed to get out of my own head for a while. You reminded me that grief and guilt don't belong to one person alone."

Paige remained in her office far into the evening. She shuffled notes back and forth. Though the notes weren't necessary, it helped to see her thoughts on paper, but nothing jumped out at her. Instead, her thoughts were keeping pace with the rhythm of shifting papers into a different order and starting the process again.

The same question kept circling around in her mind: Why now?

Paige knew she was missing something. Something that would explain what was happening. And why.

Extensive training on analyzing evidence in the ATF didn't help with this job. It was motive she and Liam needed to pin down. Paige brooded over the visit with

Reva. Something felt off there, but she couldn't identify what it was.

A knock at the door had her calling out, "Come in."

Shelley stood there, one arm laden with a bag of toys and the other hand holding three-year-old Chloe's.

"I know I'm a tough boss," she said, "but I don't expect you to work past midnight."

"Caught. You're here late, too," Paige observed.

"Later than I intended," Shelley said on a tired sigh. "Chloe's with me because Caleb's out of town and Tommy's at a friend's house. I'm on my way out," she said, depositing the bag on a chair, "but I wanted to check in with you and see what kind of progress you're making with the McKenzie case."

"Not as much as I'd like." Paige gestured to the notes she didn't need. "We've stirred up somebody enough to make two more attempts on Liam's life, and this time they weren't even disguised as accidents."

"Sounds like you're getting close."

"I wish we were." Paige proceeded to fill her boss in on what had taken place.

"We interviewed Mr. Howard, the father of Liam's best friend. He doesn't ring as a suspect for me," she said and explained about the man's wife. "We also interviewed Pope's wife—or Hawkins, as she goes by now. She's a piece of work and made no bones about how she feels about the survivors. According to her son, she couldn't do anything even if she wanted. Unless I miss my guess, she has a bad case of arthritis.

"We also talked with Reva Thomas. Her sister died in the accident, and she was on the bus as well, so she has a double connection. She was friendly enough, but not much help. And we saw Sam Newley's brother, Jerry. He couldn't add anything, either."

"I've heard of Reva Thomas. Mayor of Willow Springs, isn't she?" Shelley said. "Making a name for herself."

"That's right. With an eye to bigger things."

"You have plenty of suspects."

Paige continued her brooding. "Revenge doesn't explain the timing of the killings. If it were as simple as that, the murders would have started shortly after the accident. Revenge might play a part, but there's something larger at stake here. Something worth killing for."

Chloe started to fuss, and Shelley lifted her into her arms, murmuring to her all the while. "We're going in a minute, princess." To Paige, she said, "Let me know if you need reinforcements. In the meantime, I've got to get the princess here home. She didn't get a nap today, and it's showing."

Chloe uttered a protest that sounded dangerously close to dissolving into tears.

"It's okay," Shelley said. "We're going home."

Paige stood and brushed the hair from Chloe's face. "Princess Chloe is getting prettier every day."

"And she knows it. She has Caleb twisted around her little finger. There's nothing he wouldn't do for her."

Apparently satisfied that all was well, Chloe now chattered happily, causing Paige to smile at the idea of the tiny girl riding herd over her rough-and-ready ex–Delta soldier father. Caleb was also an operative at S&J. He could put down a perp without breaking a sweat but was sweetly tender with Tommy, the nephew he and Shelley had adopted, and Chloe. His and Shelley's family wasn't a traditional one, but it overflowed with love and laughter.

"You sound happy."

"I am."

Paige was aware that she sounded wistful and did her best to bank the feeling. She didn't begrudge Shelley her happiness one bit; she only wished she could claim some of the same for herself.

The sympathetic look that Shelley sent her way told Paige that her boss understood. Not for the first time, Paige thought how grateful she was to have a boss who was also a friend.

"It will happen for you someday. You have to be patient."

"Someday might never come." Paige cleared her throat. "Sorry. Didn't mean to whine."

"You're not whining. You're lonely for family."

Paige forced a laugh. "The last time I heard from either of my parents was a year ago at Christmas." The calls from her mother and her father, who lived a continent's distance apart, were as forced as her laugh. She'd been only too glad to get off the phone with them. Pretending that they had any kind of relationship was not only painful, it was also exhausting. She didn't doubt they felt the same.

"There's all kinds of family. S&J is your family, too. And we're grateful you're a part of it."

"Thank you, but I'm afraid I'm letting S&J and Liam down."

Shelley touched Paige's hand. "You're a first-rate operative. You've never let S&J down. And you haven't let Liam down."

Paige's lips twisted. "No. Just the ATF and my fiancé."

"Enough of that." Shelley's sharp tone had Paige looking up in surprise. "You're feeling sorry for yourself, and that isn't like you. You're smart and capable. You've had some bad breaks. Who hasn't? So get out there and do your job."

Paige stared at her boss. Shelley had never spoken to her like that before. It shook her down to her core.

"You're right. I was feeling sorry for myself." Self-pity didn't solve anything, and she detested that she found herself falling into that trap. That wasn't like her.

"You've worked difficult cases before. Why are you so afraid now?"

"I'm afraid that I'll make a misstep and get Liam killed."

Shelley stared at her with compassion. "Like your fiancé was killed? That wasn't your fault. You were cleared of any wrongdoing."

"Whose fault was it then? If I had been faster, smarter, Ethan might not be dead. I don't think I could bear it if Liam died because I wasn't good enough, smart enough, fast enough to stop it."

"What makes you think you're in control?" Shelley asked. "The last time I checked, it was the Lord who was in control. Not you."

A cry on Chloe's part had Shelley saying, "We'd better go. She's been here all day while Caleb's been on assignment. We've both had it."

Humbled, Paige acknowledged that Shelley was right. The Lord *was* in control, not her, but Paige had a responsibility to do her best. What if her best wasn't good enough? What if her best got Liam killed?

Liam drove home, his thoughts centered on Paige and what she had shared with him about her fiancé's death. Not for the first time, he found himself in awe of her strength and her faith.

He might never accept or understand her belief in the Lord's love, but he respected it and even wished he could find it for himself. His thoughts slid to the time when he'd been a believer. He'd been a regular Bible-carrying churchgoer, not just on Sunday but during the week, as well. He'd even taught a youth class, sharing his testimony and praising God at any opportunity. Now he didn't even own a Bible, much less read from it.

He rolled his shoulders, trying to relieve the tension that had gathered there. Twenty-four-hour shifts, even forty-eight-hour and longer ones, hadn't fazed Liam while he'd been on deployment. Action made the difference. Now, as he and Paige had gone over the same information again and again, he was beyond exhausted.

Rest was as important as any weapon in a soldier's arsenal. Over the last weeks, he'd skimped on sleep and was now paying for it. He was ready for a bite to eat and then sleep.

But he wasn't ready for what he found there.

Crude writings defacing the front door and sprayed on the windows should have prepared him for the ruin inside. But they didn't. How could anything have prepared him for the total destruction of his home?

It was the senselessness of the act that caused him to see red. Why?

Nails digging into his palms, he walked through the lower level of the house. Pictures of him and Jonah had been torn from their frames and ripped to pieces. Shattered glass littered the floor. Green and purple paint had been splashed over cabinets and counters, the resulting mix somehow obscene.

Plants had been overturned. Whatever lowlife had done this had mixed water with the spilled potting soil, turning it to mud. That, in turn, had been smeared over the walls and furniture, along with streaks of red that resembled blood. Even Jonah's artwork had not escaped the destruction, with filthy language defacing the pictures.

Liam picked up a picture and looked at what had been a drawing of Jonah and himself. He recalled the day

Jonah had brought it home from preschool, so proud that he'd drawn the two of them.

His innocent pleasure in his creation had filled Liam with a rush of happiness and love for his son. There was no way the picture could be salvaged.

What was he to say to his son? How did he explain the unexplainable?

Liam clenched his fists as rage poured through him. Whoever had done this would pay. The silently made promise echoed through his mind.

They'd pay dearly.

Though Liam rarely cried, tears pricked his eyes now. He didn't wipe them away.

TEN

"Are you all right?" Paige recognized the foolishness of her question. Of course he wasn't all right.

Liam had called her right after he'd called the police. He'd told her that she didn't need to come, but she'd ignored that and raced to his house. If he hadn't been out at the time, he could have been hurt, but she knew it wasn't that that filled him with rage.

It was the knowledge that his son could easily have been in the house when the vandals attacked. If Liam hadn't had the foresight to send Jonah to his grandparents', the little boy might have been hurt. Or worse.

She had arrived to find a police car, lights flashing, outside the house. Inside, one officer was busy taking pictures, while another took notes as he interviewed Liam.

Paige kept out of the way and did her own survey of the devastation. What she saw caused her gut to clench.

Vandalism was always senseless, but this took it to a new level. There'd been no need to destroy precious family pictures and a child's artwork, no need to write obscenities on the walls, no need to overturn plants and smear the dirt into the carpet.

"What about the rest of the house?" the officer asked Liam.

"I haven't looked."

"Maybe you'd better do that right now."

Liam climbed the stairs to the second floor, Paige right behind him. His bedroom appeared untouched, but when he came to Jonah's room, he stopped cold.

She stepped around him. What she saw caused her to gasp. The mattress had been slashed, the bedding tossed on the floor with what looked like blood covering it. She sniffed, confirming her guess. It was blood. Aside from being smeared on the bedding, it had also been used to write a message on the mirror: *Back off or else.*

"Liam, you don't have to look any further," Paige said quietly. "Let me take care of this."

"My son. My home. My responsibility." Systematically, he went through Jonah's room, then his own, looking for anything missing.

When he couldn't find anything, Paige knew he felt no relief. Whoever had done this had wanted to make a point that left no room for doubt as to its meaning.

"We called CSU. They'll dust for fingerprints," the older officer said. "Vandals aren't known for being careful. They might have left some behind."

Paige and Liam exchanged looks. They both knew this wasn't an ordinary case of vandalism. This was a direct warning. There'd be no fingerprints, no evidence of any kind.

A crime scene unit showed up, dusted for prints. "We'll need yours and your son's," a technician told Liam, "for elimination."

"I had my son's prints taken in an antikidnapping initiative the police held last year," Liam said. "Mine are on file with the military."

"Got it."

When the police and CSU techs left, Paige did another

survey. Unable to help herself, she picked up a picture of Jonah. It had been ripped from its frame with a bull's-eye drawn in marker on the center of his forehead.

Its message terrified her. This wasn't simply an attack on the house but a personal warning, hitting Liam where he was most vulnerable.

Liam took the picture from her, crumpled it in one large hand, then smoothed it out and laid it on the one end table that hadn't been overturned. When he looked up, there were tears in his eyes.

He made an angry swipe at them. "That's the second time tonight I've found myself crying. Deltas don't cry." He sounded bewildered as well as embarrassed.

She brushed away the remaining tears with the pads of her thumbs. "But fathers do."

He took her hand in his and brought it to his lips. "Thank you." As though suddenly aware of what he'd done, he released her hand.

"Whoever did this, we'll get them," she promised. "They won't get away with it."

"How do you know it's a them?"

"This took coordination and planning. Someone knew when you wouldn't be home and made certain this would be waiting for you. This kind of destruction took time."

"You're right. I should have figured that out for myself. Thank you for coming. I didn't know who else to call."

"You did the right thing. Now, what can I do?"

"In the morning, I need to call my insurance agent, get someone out here to take pictures. The whole thing makes me tired and it hasn't even started yet."

"Let me deal with the insurance. And I'll arrange for a cleanup crew once the agency has had time to assess the damage. I can order replacement furniture online and have it delivered."

"You don't have to—"

"I want to."

"You didn't sign on for that."

"I signed on to help you put an end to what's going on. To my way of thinking, this is part of the job."

"Thank you." His voice choked. "Seriously, thank you."

"You don't have to thank me. It's all part of the S&J service."

That wasn't true, and they both knew it. But for now, it was enough.

"There's something you need to think about," she said. "This was a direct warning, not only against you but against Jonah. Someone wants you off this case. You can step back. I'll keep investigating. I won't stop until I find who's behind all this."

"I've thought about it." The admission came with such reluctance that she longed to remove the burden from him. "But if I back off, I'd never be able to trust myself again."

She hadn't expected anything different, but she'd had to try. "Okay. I think you need to tell your parents what's going on so that they'll be extra careful with Jonah's safety."

"You're right."

After getting the name of Liam's insurance agency, she contacted it and arranged for an agent to be at Liam's house first thing in the morning.

She felt his frustration, knew he wanted to be doing something. "I know you want to clean things up, but we have to hold off. The agent will want to take pictures so the company can assess the damage."

"I know. It's not the stuff that bothers me. That can be replaced. It's the little things like Jonah's artwork.

What am I going to tell him happened to the pictures he was so proud of?"

"We'll find a way." She used the plural *we* without even thinking about it.

"Thanks. I don't think I could have faced this alone."

"You would. You could. But you don't have to. I'll be here. But there's Somebody more important on your side."

Resignation was heavy in his voice. "You're talking about God."

"And you don't want to hear it. I get it."

"It's not that I don't want to hear it. It's that God doesn't want anything to do with me. He hasn't for a long time."

"Since the accident," she said.

"Yeah. Since the accident. Maybe I'd have worked through my feelings about that, but I've seen too much, done too much to believe that the Lord even knows I'm alive."

"I'm sorry."

"Don't be." The harsh order caused her to take an involuntary step back.

"I'm still sorry. Sorry that you've been hurt so much, seen so much, felt so much that you can't believe anymore."

There was more she wanted to say, but an edgy tension shimmering from Liam warned her to hold her tongue. She let the silence settle until she thought he was ready to talk.

"You can tell me what you're feeling," she invited. "I don't bite."

"No. You don't bite. But you're probably judging me."

"Why would I do that?" Astonishment had her staring at him.

"Because I'm not a believer."

"Wow. That's pretty insulting that you think I'd judge you for not believing as I do." A line of heat rode up her spine.

"Sorry. I didn't mean… I don't know what I mean." The impatience in his words caused her to let go of much of her indignation, because she knew it was directed more at himself than at her. He straightened two kitchen chairs and gestured for her to sit.

"You're going to say the Lord helps you."

"No, I'm not."

He tilted his head.

"The Lord doesn't just help me. He carries me through it, because He knows that I'm not strong enough to do it on my own."

"He carries you?"

"He holds me in His arms and gives me of His strength until He knows I can stand on my own."

"Your faith never wavers, does it?"

"Are you kidding? My faith wavered plenty when my fiancé died. But then I realized that the Lord understands my weaknesses and forgives me. He knows the end from the beginning. I can't know that, but I do know that He is always there, ready to catch me when I fall." Her lips curved in a tiny smile. "Which is plenty."

She sat, rested her hands in her lap.

"You sure you want to hear this?" The doubtful look he sent her way had her hackles rising once more.

"I wouldn't ask if I didn't." She made no effort to keep the tartness out of her voice.

"I was a believer when I was a child. My mother had the whole family going to church every Sunday. We did the whole thing—Sunday school, Bible study on Thursday evenings, bazaars to raise money for a new roof for the church, to help a family who'd lost everything in a fire. It never occurred to me to *not* believe."

"And then the accident happened," she finished for him.

"Yeah. That changed everything. I started questioning God, asking why He let five innocent kids die because of a stupid mistake."

"Did you get an answer?"

"Not that I could tell. All I got were more questions. Finally, I decided that God either didn't care about His children or that He didn't exist at all." The despair in his voice reached down and squeezed her heart so painfully that she nearly cried out.

"Sometimes the Lord answers in ways that we don't immediately recognize." Even as she said the words, she called herself a hypocrite. Hadn't she asked the same questions when first Brett and then Ethan had died? Hadn't she doubted the Lord and His love for His children, especially for herself?

Once the shock had passed and grief had settled in, she'd done some weighty soul-searching. Railing against the senseless accident that had caused Brett's death and the ATF sting that had taken Ethan from her had achieved nothing. Rather than dwell on her anger, she had looked for and found a true testimony of the Savior—not the one of her childhood, but one she'd won through tears and self-examination.

Liam held up his hands as though to ward off any more words. "You're pretty remarkable, and I admire you for your belief. I just don't happen to share it. Not anymore."

"I'm sorry," she said. "I didn't mean to go on like that."

"You don't have to apologize for your beliefs. They're refreshing."

"Some people would call them naive."

He shook his head. "No. You believe out of conviction. That's not naive. That's strong. Incredibly strong."

"If we're not careful, we're going to have a mutual admiration society going on before long."

He gave her a steady look. "I can think of worse things."

Warmth suffused her, and she pulled back. Not physically, but emotionally. Her feelings were getting messy. Messy wasn't good. Messy wasn't good at all. Especially when she found herself growing more and more attracted to Liam.

An attraction she couldn't afford. She'd do well to remember that. Her schoolgirl crush on Liam was long over. And then there was the undeniable factor that the feelings she was experiencing were likely brought on by danger-fueled adrenaline, an emotional response that couldn't be trusted. When the case was over, the attraction would fade, and she and Liam would go their separate ways.

Which would be for the best.

She wondered why she was having such a difficult time convincing herself of it.

Paige's testimony both humbled and annoyed Liam. He couldn't share it, nor could he understand it. She was probably the smartest person he'd ever met, but she had the simple faith of a child. The two should have been a dichotomy, yet, in Paige, they fit together in perfect harmony.

The problem was that he didn't want to hear about the Lord's goodness. At one time, he would have been ashamed to admit that, but he couldn't reconcile a loving God with what he'd witnessed over the years.

"You're the strongest person I know." That was the absolute truth. He'd known plenty of heroes in his time in Delta, but Paige topped them all with her quiet belief in the Lord.

"No. I'm probably one of the weakest. But I keep going because I know I'm never alone. God is always with me."

Liam desperately wanted that belief for himself. He wanted to be able to pass it on to Jonah. But how could he? How could he, with any honesty, say he believed in God's goodness when he had seen so much, too much, of the world's ugliness?

It was a sore point between him and his parents. They held to their faith with a passionate intensity that he admired but didn't understand.

"You can have that faith for yourself. All you have to do is ask." Paige shook her head at his silence. "It's all right. I can't make you believe any more than you can make me not believe."

She left sometime after midnight. Her belief remained unshaken, while his disbelief had taken some hard knocks. Knowing he wouldn't be able to sleep, he looked through the detritus of his home, trying to decide if any of the pictures could be salvaged. Probably not.

Fortunately, he had backups of the photos on his computer, but that didn't help with Jonah's artwork. Those drawings couldn't be replaced. Jonah's pride in each piece had been palpable. Once again, Liam wondered how to explain to a five-year-old child that someone had destroyed his work.

Somewhere after four, he drifted to sleep, only to be woken by a phone call a few hours later. "Mr. McKenzie. This is Officer Mackie from last night. The lab put a rush on the blood we found in your home. It was pig's blood."

That was a relief. "Thanks for letting me know."

In the morning, an insurance agent showed up, followed by a cleaning crew.

"Mr. McKenzie, Tom Tyron from your insurance company. Paige Walker called me last night, asked if I'd handle your case personally."

"Thank you." Liam let the agent inside and showed him the wrecked room.

Tyron gave a low whistle. "Someone really did a number in here. If it's okay with you, I'll take pictures and start on a report. Good thing you didn't try to clean up. Makes it harder to assess the damage."

Liam recalled Paige's suggestion that he leave things as they were. "I probably would have, but Paige stopped me."

"She's good people. I've worked with her before. Unfortunately there are more cases like this than I want to count. If it's okay with you, I'll get started."

"Thanks."

Liam took the stairs two at a time, showered, put on fresh clothing and then decided to call Jonah. The sound of his son's voice lifted his spirits and reminded him of all that was good in the world. He spoke with his parents for a few minutes and, reluctantly, told them of the vandalism.

When he returned downstairs, he found the agent finishing up. Another ring of the doorbell announced the arrival of a cleaning crew.

"Ms. Walker called us," a friendly-looking woman said, "and told us you could use some help." She took a quick look around. "I'd say she was right. My crew will have your place spick-and-span by the day's end."

"Thank you." Liam saw the insurance agent out and, not for the first time, wondered what he'd have done without Paige.

He owed her an apology for his brusqueness last night when she'd trusted him with her feelings about God. Just because he didn't share those feelings didn't give him the right to dismiss her beliefs.

It would be empowering to believe the Lord was on his side. The reflection reminded him of his childhood, when he'd trusted God would never allow anything bad to happen.

The accident had shattered that trust. Forever.

ELEVEN

A day spent looking up the old classmates he had not yet talked with had revealed little. Several had moved away, while still others had not even heard about the accidents. Their blank expressions had convinced Liam and Paige that they were telling the truth.

As gently as possible, Liam told them of his suspicions that the deaths weren't accidents and suggested his former classmates contact the police and ask for protection. He didn't want to alarm them, but they needed to be prepared. He didn't know whether they'd seek help from the police, but he had to at least warn them.

"Something has to break loose," Paige said once they were back in the car. "We've visited all the survivors in the area, and no one popped as a murderer."

"Well, we weren't exactly expecting whoever's behind this to wear a sign saying 'Murderer,' were we?" The sharpness of his tone caused him to flush. "Sorry. I didn't mean to take it out on you."

"It's okay."

His frustration was growing with every hour.

Without any new leads, he didn't know how they were going to find out who was behind the murders, but knowing that he wasn't alone in the fight, that Paige was on his side, made a difference.

He didn't know what to make of her. She was beautiful. That was a given. She was also extremely intelligent. Another given. But there was more to this woman than he'd anticipated, and his feelings for her were more complicated than he wanted.

Simple was always best, but Paige Walker was not a simple woman. She was multilayered and complicated and so lovely that she took away his breath. Added to that were her compassion and faith and humor and everything else that went to make her up.

What right did he have to think she could want a man like him, broken in so many ways?

With more effort than it should have taken, he forced himself to turn his thoughts to what mattered: Who was next on the killer's list? And, more importantly, how could he and Paige stop another murder?

The call came as Liam and Paige drove back to his home.

"Reva. Slow down. Say that again." Liam listened with growing concern.

Her words came in bits and pieces. "A gas leak at my house… Fire department and police came." A pause as though she were trying to recall something. "A detective named Reineke showed up."

"Are you all right?" He listened some more.

"Got out in time… In hospital now."

"Okay. Get checked out. Stay overnight if they tell you to. We'll stop by to check on you." He ended the call and turned to Paige.

"Reva's house was filled with gas. The fire department got there in time. Turns out the pilot light had been turned off."

"Another so-called accident," Paige guessed.

"She's going to the hospital now. I told her we'd go see her. But first I want to check with Detective Reineke. Reva said he was at the house. Okay with you?"

"Let's go."

Liam drove to Reva's home to find the scene a jurisdictional nightmare, with the fire and police departments each vying for authority. Pouring rain didn't help matters. Police and firefighters alike wore slickers over their uniforms, making it hard to distinguish who was who.

Liam spotted the detective, who motioned him and Paige to one side.

"Gas leak. The mayor's fortunate she woke in time to get out and call the fire department. Another few minutes and it would have been a different story. Gas inhalation could have killed her."

"An accident?" Paige said with ironic emphasis.

Reineke favored her with a scowl. "It *could* be an accident. Or it could be attempted murder." His sigh was long-suffering.

"Where do we go from here?"

"I'm going to go through the records of the other 'accidents,' see what the forensic team can come up with. I'll start interviewing the remaining survivors, gather impressions. And I want to take a long look at the bus accident of fifteen years ago."

It wasn't lost on Liam that the detective was now more willing to look into things when he hadn't been earlier. Because the mayor of Willow Springs was now involved?

Reineke speared Liam with a hard look. "I'll say it again—stay out of this. You're in over your heads.

You two almost got yourselves killed, same as Mayor Thomas."

"Reva wasn't investigating anything," Liam reminded him. "There was no reason to try to kill her because of that. She was on the bus that day, same as me, same as the others who've died. As for me staying out of this, not going to happen." He returned the detective's look with a hard one of his own.

"Without Liam, you would never have connected these deaths," Paige put in quickly. "You need him." She paused. "Make that you need *us*."

"Point taken."

"We can come in tomorrow," Liam offered. "I'm willing to share what I know if you're willing to listen."

Reineke gave a grudging nod. "Fair enough."

"Paige and I are heading to the hospital to check on Reva. We'll be in around eleven in the morning, if that works for you."

"I'll be expecting you." The detective turned away to answer a question from one of his officers.

A few minutes later, Liam and Paige were on their way to the hospital. Rain blurred the windshield, the wipers working double time, their swish-swish motion a counterpoint to his thoughts.

Someone had tried to kill Reva. Would she have been next on the list anyway, or had his and Paige's visit spurred the killer to make a preemptive move on her? Guilt weighed heavily on his shoulders. Had something he'd done caused this?

"What happened to Reva—what almost happened— wasn't your fault," Paige said.

"How did you—never mind. We don't know that."

"If the killer is going after everyone on the bus that

day, he would have gotten to her eventually. The important thing is that she's all right."

As usual, Paige was right.

"I think Reineke's finally coming around," she added.

"It just took another almost-murder to get his attention." Liam gave a short laugh. "Sorry. I'm afraid Detective Reineke and I aren't going to become fishing buddies any time soon."

"It could have gone the other way if she hadn't woken up when she did," Paige mused aloud.

"Yeah. Let's get to the hospital. I want to see for myself that she's really all right."

They found Reva's room and were admitted by a nurse who couldn't have been more than five feet tall. Despite her small stature, she stared at them with a take-no-prisoners glint in her eyes. Hands planted on her hips, she glared at Liam and Paige.

"Five minutes. That's all I'm allowing anyone," she said. "My patient needs her rest. I don't care if you're the queen of England, you ain't getting more than five minutes, so don't bother arguing. Just so you know, I'm trained in martial arts and don't mind using them."

"Yes, ma'am," Liam said meekly. She sounded so much like his drill sergeant in basic training that he nearly saluted.

"Did I see you quaking in your boots?" Paige teased as the nurse marched away with a military bearing that would put many recruits to shame.

"I came close. She could give some sergeants I know lessons in intimidation." He knocked and received a faint "come in."

Inside the room, they saw a pale Reva lying on the bed. Her hair was pulled back from a face devoid of makeup. The vibrancy she'd exhibited earlier was conspicuously absent.

She lifted a limp hand in greeting. "Liam. Paige. Thank you for coming. I appreciate it…" her voice broke, and she cast her eyes down "…more than I can say." Her breath was expelled in a trembling sigh. When she lifted her head, tears swam in her eyes.

Liam crossed the room to stand beside the bed and took her hand in his. "You look a little the worse for wear."

She gave a watery chuckle. "Just what every woman wants to hear. I don't see a future in politics for you, Liam."

He grinned. "Probably not." He thought of what had almost happened, and his grin disappeared. "I'm just glad you're alive."

"So am I." Her fervent words were hoarse.

"Can you tell us what happened?" Paige asked.

Reva pressed her lips together and made a humming noise. "I stayed late to talk with my campaign manager. We discussed a few things, then I headed home. I had a bite to eat, settled down on the couch to go over some papers. I must have drifted off. Something woke me up, and I smelled gas. I called 911 and hustled out of the house."

"Do you remember what woke you?" Liam asked.

She shook her head and frowned.

Paige leaned in a bit. "Is it normal for you to fall asleep on the sofa?"

The frown deepened with what might have been annoyance. "No. I just felt extra sleepy." Reva put a hand to her heart. "When I think how close I came to dying…"

Liam saw her shake with a sudden sharply drawn breath. Almost dying tended to do that to a person.

"You take care of yourself. We'll see you later."

* * *

Outside, rain pummeled Liam and Paige as they made a beeline for the car. The howl of the wind imbued the darkness with a menacing air. An unnerving sense of being watched feathered the fine hairs at the nape of her neck. The shiver that raced down her spine did not come from the cold alone.

Her hand shielding her eyes from the pelting rain, she peered through the night, trying to identify the source of the danger.

A loud popping noise had her ducking for cover. The sound was unmistakable: a semiautomatic spitting out bullets with terrifying speed.

She and Liam sought safety behind a parked car and drew their weapons. "I can't see anything," Paige said.

"Me, either."

More shots were fired in their direction. Did the shooter have NVGs? She'd give anything for a pair of night-vision goggles right now.

"Liam!" A figure darted closer. At this distance, she could see well enough to glimpse him moving in on their right flank. "Draw his fire and I'll take him out."

"Okay."

Liam sent off a volley of shots. Under his cover fire, Paige rose and got off a shot, hitting the shooter in the shoulder. The man fell. At the same time, shots came from a second direction. Okay, that made at least two men. She turned in that direction and took aim, but the rain blurred her vision and her shot missed.

Liam fired off more shots, but the man had retreated.

When no more shots were forthcoming, she and Liam got to their feet. They ran toward where the man she'd shot had fallen, but he wasn't there. Was she wrong in thinking she'd hit him? Sheltering her eyes from the whipping wind and rain, she thought she saw a bloodstain.

"We have to call this in," she said. "I can't wait to hear what Reineke will have to say."

As it turned out, the detective had a lot to say, including calling their behavior reckless and irresponsible.

"Did you want us to sit there like ducks waiting to be picked off?" Liam asked.

Reineke didn't bother answering. "Do you two come up with these stunts on purpose just to send my blood pressure through the roof?"

"This wasn't our idea of how to end the evening, either," Paige retorted.

"I put a rush on finding out what caused the gas leak in Mayor Thomas's home. It wasn't an accident. The safety valve was turned off and the gas line leading to her stove had been cut. You were right." The admission came on a mighty heave.

"Thanks for letting us know," Paige said.

In the end, the detective sent them on their way with a warning to stay out of trouble.

On the way back to Liam's place, Paige considered what had happened. "Who knew we'd be at the hospital at that time?"

"The same person who tried to kill Reva," Liam answered.

"Maybe."

"You don't sound too sure. Who else could it have been? Reva almost died. Whoever did it most likely wanted payback."

"She had a close call," Paige agreed. The killer had miscalculated the timing. The other murders had been staged with careful attention to detail and made to look like accidents. The execution of the attempt on Reva seemed careless, almost sloppy, as had the attacks on Liam.

Liam had also survived the attempts on his life, probably due to his Delta training. That made two people who survived the killer's attempts. Was the murderer getting desperate or had something changed? The agenda was the same—to take out the survivors—but the implementation of it had taken an abrupt 180 turn.

He gave her a sidelong glance. "Something bothering you?"

"Just thinking about the timing, of how Reva woke up just in time." Paige chewed on what had happened. Something about it troubled her.

"Maybe your God was looking out for her." There was a touch of sarcasm in his voice.

That tore Paige's mind from thoughts of Reva to her and Liam's earlier discussion about the Lord and His love for His children.

"Why does that bother you?" she asked.

"It doesn't. If He kept her alive, then I'm grateful to Him. But it's more likely just good fortune on her part."

"What about the ambush on us? Was it only 'good fortune' that saved us?"

"That and the fact that we were armed."

Paige kept her disappointment to herself. Liam had enough on his mind without her preaching to him. Uncomfortable with the idea that she might have been preaching, she struck that. She hadn't preached; she'd merely borne witness of her beliefs. If Liam took offense at that, she was sorry, but she wouldn't apologize.

Her faith in God was one thing she could never compromise on. Nor, she thought, could she accept a man into her life who rejected that belief. Where had that come from? She admired Liam, liked him—a lot—but she wasn't looking for a relationship with him or with anyone.

"Whatever the reason, I'm grateful, as well." She kept the rest of her questions about the gas leak to herself.

"There's nothing more we can do tonight."

She nodded absently, her heart grieving over Liam's refusal to recognize the Lord's hand in what had happened.

At home, Liam reviewed the events of the evening. He knew he'd disappointed Paige in refusing to acknowledge the Lord's protection. Why hadn't he just agreed with her? Was his heart so steeped in bitterness that he couldn't accept even the possibility that the Lord had saved Reva from inhaling too much gas and then Paige and himself from the gunmen?

It shamed him that he had turned so far from the beliefs of his childhood. Was that what he wanted for Jonah?

No!

He wanted his son to believe in God, to have a real relationship with Him. That made him the worst kind of hypocrite.

For the first time in many years, Liam got to his knees and prayed. The words came haltingly at first, then more quickly as he poured out his heart to the Lord. After the rush of words, he waited.

For what?

A confirmation, he supposed, that the Lord had heard his prayer, but there were no blinding lights or a voice telling him that all would be okay. Instead, a quiet peace filled him. He remained on his knees, absorbing that peace.

Long minutes later, he headed to bed. The sleep he sorely needed didn't come, though, as he recalled Paige's question of who knew they would be at the hospital at that time.

It had to be the person responsible for the gas leak in Reva's house, the same individual behind all the attacks. Nothing else made sense. No one else had known he and Paige would be there at approximately that time, and nobody else would have reason to target them.

Once again he was thankful for Paige's efforts in restoring his home to normal. The ruined furniture had been removed, the walls painted, everything thoroughly scrubbed. New furniture was arriving within the week.

She had gone far beyond the parameters of her job. She'd offered her help with no thought of herself. He thought of his own job. Designing software had been fulfilling, but he wanted more. He wanted to do more, to help others the way Paige did.

Was joining the US Marshals the answer? He was beginning to think it was.

When he went to sleep, it was with a hopeful heart.

But morning brought a new set of questions with the arrival of a text.

When Paige showed up, he handed her his cell phone. "Someone sent me a text claiming to have information about the murders and wants to meet." He watched as she scrolled through the lengthy message with its directions to a location forty-five minutes away. You'll find a trailer. Go inside and wait, the text concluded.

"A setup," Paige said at once.

"I wouldn't be surprised, but we can't afford to ignore anything."

"You're right. I just don't like anonymous notes."

"I agree. Look, if you don't want to go—"

"I thought we'd been through this. Let's do it."

Following the directions given in the text, they reached the appointed area in less than forty minutes.

They found the trailer, which was little more than a rusted-out bucket, but it managed to contain the necessities, including a sink, stove, table and bed. Liam pushed open a narrow door and found a cramped bathroom that looked like it hadn't been cleaned in months. He opened a cupboard in the kitchen, closed it. "Not much here to see."

"No. But someone is living here." She pointed to a dirty cup and saucer in the minuscule sink.

A feeling of foreboding swept over him. Liam lifted his head, sniffed the air. "Smell that?"

"Propane," they both said at once.

He tried the front door and found it locked from the outside. "Check the back."

Paige ran to the back. "It's locked, too." She rammed a shoulder against the door. It wasn't just locked—something was wedging it shut.

Two propane tanks had flanked the side of the trailer. If they caught fire, they'd blow in a second. His fears were confirmed when he caught sight of a darkly clad figure creeping around the trailer. If the individual threw a match...

"Stand back." He threw himself at the door.

It didn't budge.

Again.

Same result.

"Get on my back. We're getting out of here. Now."

She did as he instructed and climbed onto his back. With their combined weight, he managed to break down the door. Outside, he didn't set her down but kept running until they reached the forest line.

Just as they ducked behind the trees, the trailer exploded. Flames shot into the air as the fire ignited the propane. Succeeding explosions continued until only the fire remained.

One more minute inside the trailer and he and Paige would have been toast.

Paige swiped at the sweat pouring down her arms. "You saved my life. Again."

"I'm thinking it was a team effort."

"All the same, thanks." She checked her cell for service. "We've got to call this in."

"I wish we'd found something."

"All we know for certain is that someone wanted us dead."

Relief shuddered through him that they had identified the odor and gotten out in time.

They checked out what was left of the trailer. Its blackened door lay to the side, a crowbar threaded through the handle. No wonder it hadn't budged when he had kicked it.

Someone had tried to murder them.

Paige fisted her hands on her hips. "We were set up."

"Yeah. But who did it?"

That question stuck in his mind as they waited for the police to arrive. It always came back to that.

Detective Reineke arrived, along with two black-and-white units.

"You two sure have a way of riling folks," he observed.

"Riling folks is what you call having someone try to kill us and almost succeeding?" Liam challenged, pointing to the crowbar wedged into the door handle. "Is that proof enough for you?"

"Look, Mr. McKenzie and Ms. Walker, I'm sorry our department didn't take you more seriously at first, but we're on the case now. Trouble is, you haven't given us much to go on. As far as that crowbar goes, we'll take it in, check for fingerprints, but I'm not expecting to find anything."

Liam faced him unflinchingly. "I'm not expecting you to find anything, either."

"What caused you to come out here in the first place?"

"We got a note." He pulled up the text on his phone and showed it to Reineke.

The detective took a picture of it. "Our CSU folks will go over the trailer, take apart what's left of it, but I don't expect to find much."

Liam gestured to the door with the crowbar wedged in the handle. "We weren't meant to walk away from this."

"All the more reason for you to leave the investigating to us."

"You refused to believe us, so we investigated on our own. This was an ambush."

"I'm still looking for a motive."

Paige got in Reineke's face. "Liam's given you the motive. Someone is picking off the survivors of that bus accident. We don't know all the ins and outs of it yet, but the connection is clear."

"I'm still not sold on it. I'll grant you that you and Mr. McKenzie have someone who's trying to kill you, but these attacks haven't been made to look like accidents. Wasn't that your theory? That the killer was making the killings look like accidents? If that's the case, why hasn't he—or she—kept to the script?"

"The first attack on Liam was made to look like an accident," Paige pointed out. "It was only when he really started investigating that the attacks escalated." She sent Reineke a scathing look. "Seems to me that it should be obvious to you that the killer is getting desperate because we're getting close to the truth."

He flushed. "You're right, ma'am. I should have seen that."

"Mr. McKenzie, Ms. Walker," Reineke continued, "you're dealing with someone who's proven he doesn't mind killing. You're both fortunate to be alive. Let the police take it from here. I promise that we won't drop the ball. By the way, a body was found not far from the hospital. There was a bullet in the man's shoulder, but that wasn't what killed him. He took a double tap to the forehead, probably a nine millimeter. Can't be sure, since the bullets were jacketed." The detective divided a look between them. "I can see that I'm not getting anywhere. All I can do is to warn you to be careful." He stomped off.

Liam recalled the terrifying moments of nearly being trapped in the trailer, but it wasn't fear that washed through him now.

It was fury.

TWELVE

The rest of the day was spent making yet another statement at the police station. That took longer than it should have as Liam and Paige did their best to convince Detective Reineke yet again that the attacks were related to the accident.

He'd come around in time, but time was something they didn't have.

When Liam received a call, he frowned at the unfamiliar number on the display before answering.

"We have your son."

His first thought upon hearing the electronically distorted voice was that someone was playing a cruel joke on him. Jonah was safe with his parents. In Savannah. No one knew he was there but Paige and her boss, Shelley Judd. There was no way they would have leaked the information, but a determined individual would find it relatively easy to figure out where he had taken Jonah.

Instinctively, he looked at Paige. The worry in her eyes echoed his own.

"What are you talking about?"

"Your son. Cute little boy named Jonah. You think he's with your parents, right?" The caller named his parents, their address. "Go ahead, call them. I'll call back in five minutes."

Hands trembling, Liam called his parents. His mother answered at once. "Jonah's missing. We've had the police here. At first we thought he had just wandered away, but…" Her voice broke.

Liam spared a precious minute to reassure first her, then his father, that he would get Jonah back. "I've got to keep the line clear," he said tersely and ended the call.

He hit the record function on his phone. The kidnapper called back exactly five minutes after they'd first talked. "If you want to see your son alive, stop your investigation into the accidents. Jonah will be released when we're satisfied that you've obeyed our instructions. Do as you're told and you'll see your son again. Easy-peasy." The voice was straight from a nightmare.

The call was disconnected.

Though both he and Paige knew there was little to no possibility of tracing it quickly and without a warrant, she called S&J and asked if the firm's IT person could run a reverse-trace program. This might not be possible, since they were almost positive this was a virtual number, which meant no one could see the caller's real number.

Liam listened as Paige explained the situation to the S&J operative, but, inside, he shook with terror. He couldn't give in to it. Coldness such as he'd never known invaded him. Were it possible for his blood to turn to ice, it would have at this moment. His insides tightened with such force that he felt like he couldn't breathe.

"I did this. If I hadn't been so arrogant, thinking that I could keep Jonah safe and continue the investigation, my son would be home with me right now. If something happens to him…" He stopped, unable to put what came next into words. Waves of guilt-tainted fear washed over him.

Get a hold of yourself, man. The bracing words did nothing to banish the unbearable horror of knowing his son was in the hands of a murderer, though.

"The person who took Jonah is to blame. Not you. We don't know that the threats against you and Jonah would stop even if you backed off. Someone is playing a very dangerous game, and since you're one of the survivors, they wanted you dead before you started investigating."

"In the unit when we faced something horrific, we were taught to ignore and override. How do I ignore my son's kidnapping? How do I override that?" His voice rose with every word. The shouted words stunned because they came from him.

He paced across the room, back and forth, clenching and unclenching his hands, as if the motion itself would bring Jonah home safely.

Losing control wasn't like him. It wasn't like him at all. He took a breath. Another. When he had himself under control, he asked, "What do we do now?"

"Do you have a record function on your phone?"

He nodded. "Jonah and I have a game where I leave a message for him on the phone, record it, and then he can play it back as many times as he wants."

"Good. I want to hear the call again. We can't tell anything from the voice—it's too heavily processed—but maybe the words themselves will tell us something."

Liam hit the playback function, and they both listened to the chilling message.

"'Easy-peasy,'" Paige said, repeating a phrase. "We heard that not long ago."

Reva had used the words while talking about dismissing people who didn't like her. It had been a catchphrase of hers from years ago. He remembered Marie teasing her about it.

"Reva," they said in unison.

Shock shook Liam to his core, but it explained why the attack on her had failed and how the men who shot at him and Paige at the hospital knew they'd be there. Reva had set it all up, making herself appear a victim and, at the same time, using the opportunity to try to take them out.

Identifying the murderer/kidnapper had been the easy part. Finding Jonah and rescuing him was another matter.

"I want to do a run on Reva," Paige said, "especially any properties she owns. Residential and commercial."

Liam was silent for a moment. "Years ago, her father owned a paper mill operation. I don't think he ever sold it, even after the factory shut down."

Paige did a property search and found what they were looking for. "The property is still in his name. It's about a half hour from here."

She brought up a picture of the factory. "It looks to be fairly secluded. Perfect for holding a hostage. Also, she'd need a place to manufacture the things that caused the accidents. Not exactly something she could do at home."

"She may not be there," Liam pointed out. "She could have some hired guns she'd left with Jonah."

"I think she *has* to be there. She wants control of everything. It's part of who she is. If she's there—and I think she is—we'll take her down together and then find Jonah."

He shook his head. "No. I'll go in by myself. I'll keep her attention while you look for Jonah."

"Think it through," Paige said. "Reva has to be feeling desperate. Otherwise, she'd never have taken Jonah. She won't hesitate to kill you or anyone else who gets in her way. She's proved that. Let me go with you and watch your back. Besides, Reva will be suspicious if we don't go in together."

He'd already thought about that and decided it couldn't be helped. "We'll have to risk it. Finding Jonah comes first. It has to." Fear clogged his throat, making it difficult to get the words out. "You're a great operative, Paige, but you're not a parent. You don't understand what it is like to know your child is in danger and to feel helpless to do anything about it."

Liam respected Paige's abilities, but he'd spoken only the truth. She wasn't a parent and couldn't imagine the terror he was going through. What right did she have to tell him what to do?

"You're right," she said. "We'll do it your way."

He lifted a brow. "You're giving in? Just like that?"

"No. Not just like that. I'm saying that we'll do it your way because it's your son. It has to be your decision."

"Thank you."

She crossed the room and wrapped her arms around him. She didn't say anything, only held him.

"I'm here," she murmured against his chest. "And I'm not going anywhere."

As Paige closed her arms around him, warmth seeped into him, banishing some of the brutal cold that had overtaken him when he'd received the call.

How had she known that he just needed to be held? Her arms were strong, her breath sweet as it fanned his face. The knowledge that she was on his side bolstered his own flagging courage.

Nothing had ever scared him the way this had. He'd faced down terrorists determined to kill him, had fast roped from a helicopter in the middle of the night to a ship bobbing in the ocean and had parachuted out of a plane miles above the earth. He'd done all that and more, but none of it compared to the gut-wrenching fear of knowing his son was in the hands of a murderer.

If he lost Jonah… He didn't finish the thought. Couldn't. Not if he wanted to keep any measure of sanity.

"We'll get Jonah back," Paige said. The certainty in her voice calmed his nerves, and he held on to it as he would a lifeline. "We're not alone. The Lord is on our side."

She was right. He felt the Lord's presence. How had he ever doubted it? The Lord had been with him when he'd returned again and again to save his friends trapped in the bus. He had also been with him in the horror of war, bringing him home safely. And the Lord was with him now.

He wanted to tell Paige of his feelings, but now wasn't the time.

Gently, he set her away from him. "Let's do this."

"If you're ready."

"I'll never be ready for seeing my son in danger, but I'm ready to do whatever I need to get him out of it."

For Liam, that said it all.

As he had done before every op, he wiped his mind clean of worry. Worry never helped and often hindered. Instead, he let his thoughts wander to past Delta ops, bringing up the distinct whir of an MH-60 Black Hawk helicopter, the black Nomex uniforms he and his teammates wore, the feel of an assault rifle strapped to his shoulder. He had none of those here, only the H&K USP pistol at his side and a folding knife, a Benchmade 9050 automatic with its lethal needle-thin point, concealed in his boot.

He considered calling Reineke and letting him know what was going on, but he still didn't fully trust the detective after he'd been so dismissive.

On the plus side, though, he had a partner who had proved herself over and over. He'd worked with some of the best operators in the business, and Paige outshone them all. He'd go into battle with her any day.

Focused on what needed to be done, he regulated his breathing. The familiar routine was comforting. He knew he could depend upon Paige to get Jonah out. All he had to do was face down a murderer who had shown she had no problem killing anyone who got in her way.

The drive to the factory was made in grim silence. What was there to say? Paige gave Liam space. That was the most she could do for him. She drove, not minding the quiet. Sometimes, silence was a gift.

From the look he sent her, he felt the same. She prayed silently. *Lord, we need You. Jonah needs You. Please get us through this. Give me the strength and wisdom to know what to do.*

More settled now, she turned to Liam, hoping he could feel the peace that prayer had given her, but the air of subdued menace that emanated from him held her tongue.

Competing thoughts crowded her mind, and the silence grew until it filled the small space. It no longer felt like a gift but was now a barrier between them. There was a quiet, desperate taste to the air. She licked her lips in an attempt to get rid of it, but it persisted.

She supposed that she should suggest that they bring in the police, the FBI, but she didn't. She already knew what Liam's response would be. As an LEO, she'd have been bound to report a kidnapping, but she was no longer a law enforcement officer and no longer had to abide by the rigid rules under which they operated.

Tension shimmered through the car, tension and that now-oppressive silence that made its own kind of noise. She tried to shake it off, but it clung like a bad smell.

Liam was an intelligent man who was in an impossible situation. If it were her child, what would she do? She honestly didn't know. How could she? The love between a parent and a child was sacred. She'd always believed that, even with the less-than-perfect relationship she had with her own parents.

She longed to reassure him that everything would be all right, that they would get Jonah back unharmed, but she couldn't in good faith make those promises. Right now, Liam needed her skills as an agent, not the feelings of a woman, but she was both, and it was becoming increasingly difficult to separate the two.

What was she supposed to do with those feelings? They were messy and unwieldy and altogether unwanted. Honesty forced her to admit that the last wasn't totally true.

By the creases between his brows, she knew that in his mind Liam was already in the factory, confronting Reva and plotting how to take her, along with any henchmen she might have with her, down.

It didn't help that she had the feeling he wanted to say something and then clamped his lips shut. When he finally spoke, it was a relief, though the words were rough and uneven. "We don't know what we'll be walking into. You don't have to do this."

"That's the dumbest thing I've heard in a long time."

"Sorry. Maybe I should just say thank you."

"Maybe you should."

"Thank you for that and for not saying we should have called the police."

"I thought about it," she admitted.

"But you didn't. So, thanks." The gruff tone was so filled with fear and pain that she wondered they both didn't drown in it.

"I know how you feel," she said. "Reineke may be

okay, but he hasn't exactly shown himself to be on our side." She thought of ops with the ATF. "Also, the more people involved, the more things that can go wrong."

Silence filled the car again.

They parked a distance from the factory and made their way through a heavily wooded forest.

Paige patted her vest. Flash-bangs. Flexicuffs. Several lengths of rope. A snack for Jonah. Her Glock was in the shoulder holster, her clutch piece tucked in one boot. She hoped she wouldn't have to use any of the weapons, especially in front of Jonah.

The abandoned factory lived up to the reputation of such buildings. An eerie atmosphere surrounded it. Heavy steel doors and barred windows gave it a forbidding air. Desperately she searched for another plan, something that didn't involve Liam walking into the factory alone. She'd find a back way in and locate Jonah.

She opened her mouth, intent on convincing him to let her go with him, when he put a finger to her lips.

"Get Jonah out. That's all you need to do." Hard lines bracketed his mouth. "Take care of yourself. There's probably someone with him."

"Let me go with you. We'll take care of Reva and then find Jonah. Together."

"I can take care of myself." He gave a forced smile, then tapped his chest. "Delta, remember? Do you think I can't take down one woman?"

She leaned in and touched her lips to his. "I'll take care of Jonah. You do the same with yourself."

"Count on it." He hesitated. "If things go south…"

She didn't give him the opportunity to finish. Instead, she stood on tiptoe to brush her lips over his. "Nothing's going wrong. We're bringing Jonah home."

She gave him a thumbs-up, wishing she felt as confident as she pretended. Jonah's life depended upon what she did next.

Liam walked into the factory without any attempt to conceal his entrance. If Reva was here, he wanted all her attention on him. The cavernous room was lit only by two naked bulbs hanging from the ceiling, giving off stingy streams of light.

He walked to the center of the room and said, "Might as well come on out, Reva. I know you're here." Automatically, he slipped into his Delta unit commander's voice.

No answer.

Had he and Paige been wrong? They'd followed a hunch, a reasonable one, but it was a hunch all the same.

He tried again. "I'm not surprised you're afraid to show yourself. Only a coward kidnaps an innocent child and then hides behind him."

Reva appeared from behind a stack of wooden crates. "Not very smart, speaking to the person who holds your child that way." She huffed out an annoyed breath. "You couldn't have known it was me."

Liam did his best to keep his focus on Reva rather than on the gun she held with such casual ease, but he couldn't keep his eyes off the .357 Magnum. With a short four-inch barrel, the old revolver was capable of punching a hole right through a man.

It wasn't a small gun, but she held it with an effortlessness that spoke of familiarity.

She followed his gaze. "You like my little toy? It belonged to my father. He gave it to me when he and my mother sold me the house." She shook her head at her own musings. "Enough of that. There's no way you could have known it was me."

"But I did."

"How?" Annoyance was ripe in her voice. "Come on. Admit it. You were guessing."

"You used the phrase *easy-peasy* on the phone. You're the only one I know who says that."

Chagrin crossed her face. "Two little words. That was careless on my part," she said. "And I tried to be so careful." A spiteful little smile touched her mouth as though she was reluctantly admiring a despised enemy's cleverness.

Liam stared at her in amazement. "That's what you're upset about? What about killing three people and trying to kill Paige and me and kidnapping my son?"

She snapped her fingers, the gesture clearly dismissing the lives she'd taken. "Speaking of Paige, where is your partner? You two seemed joined at the hip. Never mind. My men will take care of her."

Liam pushed back his fear for Paige and focused on what Reva was saying.

"I'm going places. I can't afford to make careless mistakes like that."

"You don't call murder a 'careless mistake'?"

"I call it a means to an end. What are the lives of three nobodies compared to mine? I'm going to make a difference in the state, then in the nation. Nothing's going to stop me."

Liam folded his arms across his chest. "That's where you're wrong."

Her smile was intolerably smug. "You? You won't stop me, because you'll be dead."

"You'd kill me?"

"Don't sound so surprised. I've tried hard enough. This time I'll make sure."

"What happened to you, Reva? You were a decent kid from a decent home. What went wrong?"

"I got smart."

"That's all you have to say. Why? Why kill our friends? Why try to kill me? You and I were friends."

"You were Marie's friend. Never mine."

"You're wrong."

He needed to keep her attention on him and give Paige time enough to find Jonah. "The gas in your house? That was you."

Reva gave a trilling laugh. "Of course. I turned off the safety valve and cut the line to the stove. Then all I had to do was fake being asleep and waking up to find my house filling with gas. I had to keep you from looking too closely at me. Becoming another victim was the easiest way to make you look in another direction."

"You could have died." Disbelief sliced through him at the risk she'd taken.

"I was safe enough. I called 911, hysterical and sobbing. Everybody bought it. Including you."

Paige hadn't, Liam thought. She'd questioned Reva's surviving the incident from the first. He should have paid attention to her doubts, but he'd been unable to see the girl he'd known from so long ago as a murderer.

"You should have left it alone," Reva said, her voice hard once more. "But, no, you had to keep digging." Fury flashed in her eyes, spilled over in an angry spate of words. "I should have known you'd be a problem and taken care of you first. Once the blackmail stopped, I would have stopped killing people. There'd be no point in it. If you want to blame someone, blame whoever is blackmailing me. That's the real culprit."

"And the people you murdered are just so much collateral damage."

"Of course. What else?" She brushed her hand through the air, dismissing killing three people. "Doesn't matter now. You're going to die, along with that son of yours and, of course, your little friend, Paige."

"You'd kill a child?"

"It's survival of the fittest. You have to be willing to do what's necessary if you're going to succeed. You were a big-time Delta operator. You should know that."

"You're sick, Reva. I wonder how I didn't see it before."

Irritation spiked in her voice. "What I am sick of is this tedious conversation."

She shrugged, the motion lifting her dark hair in a bouncy fluff.

"At least tell me why. Why kill our friends?"

"You still don't get it, do you? It was my fault that the bus went off the bridge that day."

"Your fault?" Liam shook his head. "Pope fell asleep at the wheel."

"I made him do it. Not on purpose. I wanted to stay around the school after the game. There was a boy on the other team who I wanted to notice me. So I put something in Pope's water bottle that I thought would cause him to fall asleep while we were at the game. I never thought he wouldn't use it until we were on our way back. By then, it was too late."

Liam struggled to make sense of her words. "You put a sedative in his water bottle…all so we could stick around and you could get some boy to notice you?" Even as he said the words aloud, he could scarcely believe them.

"He was on the other team. We'd flirted a bit at other games. If I had time with him, I could have gotten him to ask me out. But no. Old Goat Pope had to drink a soda

at the game. He never touched his water bottle until…
until it was too late."

"You could have said something, stopped him from
drinking it."

"What? Like, 'Hey, Mr. Pope, I doctored your water
bottle and you're gonna take a nap real soon'? If I'd
known what would happen…but I never dreamed he'd
drive the bus right off the road and into the river. I was
on the bus, too, you know.

"By the time it was over, it was too late. Those kids
died. I couldn't tell the truth then."

"Okay. But why kill the survivors now?"

"I told you. I'm being blackmailed. It has to be one of
the survivors, someone who saw me that day. I've paid
out $275,000 so far. Another payment and I'll be ruined.
I won't have enough money for my campaign, much less
anything else."

"Like fancy shoes," he murmured.

"What?"

"Nothing. Just something Paige mentioned."

"Ah, yes. Smart, smart Paige. She should have minded
her own business. Like you." Reva glanced about. "I
didn't expect she'd let you come here on your own. She
must be trying to find that brat of yours."

Liam didn't bother responding to that. He needed to
keep Reva's attention on him. "Let me guess. The blackmail started about six weeks ago." Paige had been right
all along in her conviction that Sam was connected. He
was busy putting together the pieces in his head. "You
could have refused to pay. Let the truth come out. What
you did was bad, but it wasn't murder. Manslaughter
maybe, but not murder."

"I'd be ruined personally and politically. And there
was nothing to be gained in letting everyone know what

really happened. I can't have it come out that I caused the bus accident. I can't." She said the last more to herself than to him, as though she'd had that same argument in the past, trying to convince herself of the rightness of her actions. She lifted her chin to stare at him.

Murderous rage flared in her eyes. Fear pulsed through him. Not for himself, but for Jonah and Paige.

"How about Calvin Pope? He would have been vindicated if it were proven that the accident wasn't his fault."

"Who cares about Old Goat Pope? Nobody ever liked him in the first place. Just as well he died when he did."

"And his family?"

"What about them? His old lady was a shrew, and the son was weird. They never amounted to anything fifteen years ago, and they sure don't now. You can't compare them to what I've accomplished, to what I can do for the state. And beyond."

But Liam wasn't listening to her self-aggrandized visions and looked at her incredulously. "Is that your excuse for letting Pope take the rap and destroying five families?"

"Like I said, who cares?" Reva asked in a bored tone. "But now I have to do something with you. I was afraid you and that little friend of yours were getting too close, which is why I hired those first two idiots to take you out. They failed miserably.

"If there's one thing I've learned since I've been in politics, it's that if you want something done right, you have to do it yourself." She shook her head with feigned sadness. "The work ethic of today isn't what it used to be." She looked at him thoughtfully. "You're a hard man to kill, Liam."

"Should I apologize?"

"No need. I'll feel real regret at having to shoot you, but you haven't left me any choice."

"There's always a choice."

"Don't be naive. You know everything. And how do I know that you weren't the one blackmailing me in the first place?"

"You really believe that?"

"No. Probably not. You're too much a Boy Scout for blackmail."

"That didn't stop you from trying to kill me."

"I couldn't take the risk of believing anyone innocent. Even you. I had to keep staging the accidents until the blackmail stopped. That's the only way I'd know for sure that I got the right person. It's too late to turn back now." Her voice took on an almost pleading note. "You see that, don't you? I didn't have a choice."

"Listen to yourself. You're justifying murder just to keep your secret." He didn't bother concealing the contempt in his voice.

"That secret is the only thing standing in my way of getting out of this small-potatoes town and becoming somebody. I'm going to win a seat in the state legislature and from there…who knows? Maybe a congressional seat one day. And after that? There's no limit to what I can do."

Gone was the pleading.

In its place was a haughty arrogance, accompanied by a naked hunger for power. How had he ever thought of her as Marie's harmless if annoying little sister? This was a woman convinced of her absolute right to do whatever she deemed necessary on her quest to achieve her goals, no matter who she had to kill to get there.

She aimed her gun at him. "You can buy yourself a little more time if you tell me what you have on me. It would really be a shame if I have to kill you right now."

THIRTEEN

Paige found a rear entrance.

The back of the building was a rabbit warren of hallways leading to rooms filled with manufacturing machines, their hulks casting huge shadows, each providing a hiding place for a predator. The factory stirred up whirling, churning memories of when Ethan had been killed.

Her palms grew wet, her mouth dry.

Three years of nightmares threatened to spill over and out. An inner voice shrieked at her to turn and run, but she held to her course. The only thing that kept her moving forward was that Liam was depending on her to find his son. She began the tedious process of checking each room until she heard sounds from a television coming from a room at the end of a hallway.

Approaching cautiously, she kept to the side of the hallway. The door to the room was partially open, and she saw two men tipped back in chairs, eating and watching TV. In the back of the room was Jonah on a cot, hands and feet bound. Fury rose in her, fury and a deep desire to make the men pay for their part in terrifying a little boy.

Jonah saw her, opened his mouth, but she put a finger to her lips. He nodded in understanding.

She approached as quietly as possible, then disabled the first man with a hard chop to the back of his neck.

The other man jumped up from his chair and spun around. He lunged toward her, reaching for her shoulder. She ducked under his arm and got behind him, grabbed his hand in a sophisticated joint lock, and then forced his hand back over his forearm in an aikido move she'd picked up in her close quarters battle training. She'd excelled at CQB and hand-to-hand combat and was grateful to have them in her arsenal now.

He yowled with pain as she twisted harder, bringing him to his knees. From there, it was easy enough to force him to the floor. She didn't give him time to recover but was on him and pressed her thumbs to the vulnerable spot in his neck. It was lights out for him.

Quickly, she disarmed the men, tucked their weapons in her vest, then secured their hands behind their backs with the flexicuffs she'd brought with her and tied their ankles together with lengths of rope she took from her vest.

She crossed the room to Jonah. The little boy was as cute as his pictures promised. She knew he had to be frightened and approached him slowly. "Jonah, I'm a friend of your daddy's," she said and undid the ropes binding his hands and feet. She blinked back tears upon seeing the reddened areas where the ropes had bitten tender skin. "We're here to take you home."

Hope widened his eyes. "Daddy's here?"

"Yes. We need to find a safe place for you while I go help him. Can you walk?"

"I don't know." He tried to stand, then fell back to the cot.

The binding around his ankles must have cut off his circulation. Gently, she rubbed his wrists and ankles, trying to restore feeling. Fresh anger surged through her toward the men who had done this to a child.

"New plan." She stooped down. "Can you put your arms around my neck? I'm going to give you a piggyback ride."

Jonah wrapped his arms around her neck and his legs around her waist.

She found a secluded room to put him in. "Can you be really brave for just a little while longer? Stay here and wait until I come back with your daddy?"

"I…I think so."

"Good boy. Are you hungry?"

The look in his eyes confirmed her guess, and she handed a snack to him.

"I'll be back soon," she said and went in search of Liam.

The faint hope that Reva would respond to his plea that she give herself up seeped out of him, but he kept his expression blank, unwilling to give her any more advantage over him. As long as Jonah was in danger, he couldn't make a move against her. Once Paige let him know that his son was safe, he'd act.

Why hadn't Reva attacked him? It had to be something more than wanting to know what he had on her.

And then he got it. She was basking in the glory of self-aggrandizement. She wanted, no, needed, to be praised, to be lauded, even if it was only by herself.

He realized there was a second reason. She wanted to see his fear, to feel it.

People like Reva fed on the fear of others. He'd seen it in Afghanistan, where warlords forced others to bow to their bidding by threatening to do unspeakable things to their families. Fear was a powerful motivator.

If he allowed his fear to dictate his reaction to anything Reva said, he, Paige and Jonah were as good as dead. His best bet was to keep her talking.

Reva leveled a taunting gaze at him. "You're scared, aren't you? The big, bad ex-Delta is scared of little ol' me. I love it." Her laugh rang out, the shrill tone scraping against his nerves. "Imagine my surprise and grief when it comes out that you're the one who killed those three who died in the so-called accidents. I'll shed a few tears and tell everyone that you must have just snapped from the guilt you've been carrying all these years."

"How are you going to arrange that?" he asked, going for bored. *Don't let her see she's getting to you. That only feeds her power.*

"I have friends all over, friends who can whisper to the right people that you hadn't been right in the head ever since the accident. People will speculate that you were suffering from survivor's guilt over those kids in the bus who didn't make it and took it out on the ones who did. You even hired a private security team to look into it, when all along, it was you. You didn't know what you were doing."

Liam kept his tone bored. "Ever hear of something called evidence?"

"Oh, there'll be evidence. I have the wire and other things I used to cause the accidents. They'll conveniently turn up somewhere, maybe your gym locker or a storage place you rented. These things always have a way of coming out."

He silently acknowledged that he was impressed by the glib way she presented it. Could she get enough people to believe the theory that he had been so overcome with regret and guilt that he had gone on a killing spree?

"What about the attempts on my life? How are you going to explain those away?"

"Why, you staged them, of course. What better way to divert suspicion from yourself?" Another of those trilling laughs that held not a speck of humor. "I should know. My little playacting worked out better than I'd ever dreamed. Even the governor himself sent flowers after my brush with death." Pride resounded in her voice. She motioned to her left. "Come on out."

At her command, two men, each of whom looked like he could have starred in a pro wrestling match, appeared. "Hold him."

The men took Liam's arms. He jammed his elbow in one man's gut, but the other delivered a punishing blow to Liam's kidneys. He fell to his knees, breathing heavily. Remembering the knife in his boot, he reached for it and closed his hand around its hilt.

The first man, now recovered, grabbed Liam's wrist and twisted it back, forcing him to drop the knife.

Reva came to stand closer and picked up the knife. "Nice toy. I believe I'll keep it." She made a tsking noise at Liam. "That was all so unnecessary. You may not believe this, but I don't like seeing you in pain."

"Right the first time." He grunted out the words. "I don't believe it."

Though the men hovered nearby, she held up a hand, stilling them. "You always were smart, but not as smart as that little partner of yours." She raised her voice. "I know you're here, Paige. Might as well come out."

"I came alone."

"Liar."

"Liam gets a bullet to the knee if you don't show yourself." Reva lowered the gun and pointed it at his right leg.

Paige walked out from behind one of the piles of crates. "Don't hurt him."

"Take her," Reva shouted to one of the men, who grabbed Paige by the shoulders, while his partner did the same with Liam.

Paige gave a subtle nod in his direction. He understood that she'd found Jonah and that his son was safe. Fresh energy surged through him.

"Tell me what you have on me," Reva ordered Paige. "I don't mind shooting you in the leg before I kill you. I should warn you. I'm pretty good with this thing. Daddy taught me to shoot just around the time I could tie my own shoes. Marie was never interested, but I took to it right away."

"You'll kill us either way. That's what you had in mind all the time, isn't it?" Paige asked.

Reva shrugged. "Would you rather die now or later? Makes no difference to me either way."

"I'd rather not die at all."

FOURTEEN

Paige made her move. She rammed her elbow up and back, catching the man who held her in the chin. The crack of bone told her she'd made hard contact. Blood spurted, then sprayed, its warm stickiness coating her shoulders and neck. Couldn't be helped.

Taken by surprise, he released her.

She spun so that she now faced him. The hate-filled glare in his eyes promised retribution. Too bad. She wasn't going to give him time to exact it.

"I ain't gonna take it easy on you 'cause you're a woman," he said as he wiped his chin.

"I don't expect you to."

She struck out with her foot, aiming at his chest. When that didn't faze him, she followed up with another kick, this one to his knee. That brought results as he clutched his injured leg.

He gave a guttural groan.

He moved in, and she danced away, sparing a glance to see how Liam was doing with his opponent. Liam was well over six feet, rangy with lean muscle, but his opponent had bulked-up shoulders and arms thick as tree limbs.

"Worried about your man?" her opponent taunted. "You should be. He's no match for Cable."

The Cable in question was at least six four, with arms ropy with muscle and sinew. He probably outweighed Liam by fifty pounds or more. The glint in his eyes said he was relishing the fight.

Paige put it out of her mind. Right now, she was too busy ducking fists the size of Virginia hams. A blow from them could easily knock her out.

He had a tell, a muscle in his jaw twitching, when he was about to throw a punch. She used that and came in hard and fast before he struck her, catching him in the gut with her own fists. Though she lacked his power, she had speed and agility on her side. The stunned expression in his eyes when she hit him gave her a fleeting satisfaction, but he wasn't down.

Neither was she.

She looked up, expecting to see Reva hightailing it out of there. Instead, the woman stood to one side, avid gaze riveted on the fights, reminding Paige of spectators watching battles to the death in ancient Rome.

She'd deal with Reva soon enough. Right now, she had to make her man angry enough to lose control.

"Big guy like you ought to be able to take on one puny woman. Guess you're not so tough after all, huh?"

Nostrils flaring with insult, he charged. She was ready and reversed the energy of the attack in a move known as *irimi nage*. He went down hard, his head hitting the concrete floor with a reverberating thud. She wasted no time in securing his hands in flex ties.

Liam had disabled his opponent and had him on the ground, a knee in the man's back. "Was it you and your partner who vandalized my house and threatened my son?" He yanked up the man's head.

"Yeah. So what?"

"I'm going to take special pleasure in seeing both of you put away for a long time." As Paige had with her man, Liam bound the man's hands.

The two men were out, but Reva was still very much a force to be reckoned with.

She broadened her stance, her .357 Magnum held on Paige and Liam. "Bravo. You are both to be congratulated on taking out those two fools. It's a good thing I stuck around to make sure the job was done right this time. If I'd done that earlier, you wouldn't still be around getting in my business." Without further fanfare, she fired.

Liam fell to the floor.

Paige's heartbeat faltered at seeing Liam fall. Rage such as she'd never known filled her. She advanced toward Reva when she saw Liam wink. Reva had missed the shot. Renewed hope gave her the energy she needed, so when Reva raised the revolver again, Paige didn't give her time to use it but kicked it from the woman's hand, then delivered a right cross to her jaw.

Reva was down. For her own good, Paige hoped she stayed that way.

Paige secured Reva's hands behind her. She pulled out her cell and punched in 911, gave her name and the address.

"Where's Jonah?" Liam asked.

"I'll get him." Minutes later, she returned with a frightened-looking Jonah in her arms. She set him down, and he ran to his father.

"Daddy?"

"Yeah, buddy. It's me. How 'bout a hug?"

Jonah wrapped chubby arms around Liam's neck. "You won't send me away again, will you?"

"Not on your life. I can't get along without you. You're my best buddy."

"The bad men told me that you weren't coming," Jonah said, a break in his voice, "but I knew you would. I told them that, but they just laughed."

Upon hearing that, Paige wished she could put a hurt on the men again. Wanting to give father and son time together, she gave a statement to the police when they arrived. Reineke showed up shortly after the locals. Predictably, he wanted to know why she and Liam hadn't called him when Liam first received the call regarding the kidnapping. Paige soothed ruffled feathers and explained that they weren't certain Jonah was being held at this location and that they had had to act fast if they were to save him. It was a feeble excuse at best, and she flushed. But when Reineke continued to harp on their going off on their own and not involving the police, she'd had enough.

"What would you have done if it had been your son, Detective? Would you have called the cops for backup or would you have gone after him yourself?"

That quieted his objections.

Liam, Jonah and Paige were finally allowed to leave the factory. After they had Jonah checked out at the hospital and his rope burns were treated, they returned to the house. By tacit agreement, Liam and Paige postponed any discussion about the case.

Jonah insisted that Paige stay for his favorite dinner of mac and cheese and hot dogs. Three bedtime stories and numerous glasses of water later, he was down for the count.

Working in tandem, Liam and Paige cleaned up the kitchen. When they were done, she said, "It's not over."

The killer had been caught, but the blackmailer was

still out there. Until he or she was stopped, Liam and his son would never be safe.

Liam's euphoria at being reunited with Jonah took a nosedive after he'd put his son to bed. Accumulated tension and fear had taken their toll, and he desperately wished he could put the whole thing behind him.

But Paige was right. It wasn't over.

Not yet ready to talk about what came next, he thought about Reva. "Reva was just a kid back then. How did she go so wrong? Maybe if I'd stayed in touch with her after Marie died, things would have been different."

"She made her choices a long time ago," Paige said. "They're finally catching up with her."

"'They that plow iniquity and sow mischief shall reap the same,'" he murmured, quoting a Scripture from the book of Job. It was a perfect caption for Reva's life. "I'm surprised I remembered that."

"I'm not." Paige's voice was soft. The moment hung, imbued with feelings neither was ready to give voice to.

The chirp of his phone interrupted the shimmer of feelings that remained. Liam glanced at the display and saw it was Detective Reineke. He put it on speaker so that Paige could hear.

After asking about Jonah, Reineke got down to the purpose for his call. "Ms. Thomas admits to everything except luring you and Ms. Walker to that trailer and trying to blow you up. Could be that she's lying, but I tend to believe her. Looks like you may have another enemy out there, Mr. McKenzie."

"Thanks, Detective. I appreciate you letting me know." Liam hung up and looked at Paige. "What do you think?"

"I think he's right. The blackmailer had reason to want

you dead. You stood in the way of continuing to bleed Reva for money."

"Okay," he said at last. Reva had been caught, but the person who had set the murders in motion was still out there.

"Reva said that she'd started receiving the threats six weeks ago," Paige reminded him. "Sam Newley died just around then. I keep coming back to that."

"Me, too," Liam admitted. "Sam would never have been involved in blackmail, though. It wasn't his style."

"No. I didn't know him very well, but I could see that he was a straight-arrow kind of guy. You can't deny the timing, though. Could Sam have seen Reva doctor Pope's water bottle? Maybe that's what turned him so thoughtful on the drive home."

"Sam wouldn't have let Pope take the fall for something that wasn't his fault." Liam was very certain of that.

Paige's brow dipped in thought. "Maybe he felt sorry for Reva. She was just a kid. There was nothing he or she could do to bring back the kids who died. If Pope had been in danger of going to jail, it might have been different, but he was never charged with anything."

Liam brooded over it. "That sounds like Sam," he said finally. "He always wanted to think the best of people. It was part of what made him such a good friend. Maybe he was waiting for her to come forward."

"Who would he have told?"

"At one time, he and I were tight. I think he would have come to me, but we lost touch." Liam shook his head at his neglect of their friendship. "I joined the army, then Delta. After graduating from college and medical school, Sam started his research. We both promised that we'd catch up someday, but it never happened. And then he got sick."

"What about his brother? Would Sam have told him?"

"Jerry was more than six years younger than Sam, so they were never even in the same school."

"Sam knew he was dying," Paige said slowly. "Maybe he didn't want to take that secret with him and decided he had to tell someone. Who better to tell than his brother?"

"It makes sense. Could Jerry have had the brains to pull it off?"

"Blackmail doesn't take brains so much as cunning and the willingness to do what most of us would consider unthinkable."

Liam thought about it. "How do we find out?"

Paige leaned in close. "Here's what we do."

"I don't like it," Liam said after Paige shared her plan with him.

"You don't have to like it," Paige said, her patience straining. She and Liam had been over this again and again. "You only have to go along with it. Just like I did with you when you were meeting Reva."

"Playing dirty," he muttered.

"It's simple. I call Jerry, say that I have something important to tell him. He invites me over and I give him my proposition—either he pays me or I go to the police with the information that he was the blackmailer. If we're right about him, he'll go along with it. Or he'll try to stop me. If he doesn't react, then we know we're on the wrong track, but I'm pretty sure we're right."

"And you think he's just going to let you waltz in and accuse him of blackmail?"

"No. I think he's going to deny it, then finally admit that I'm right. Just like with Reva, he'll want to boast about how smart he was, how he'd fooled everyone. I've got a digital recorder in a pin that I'll wear."

"Why don't I do it?"

"Because he'll be suspicious of you. Me?" She lifted her shoulders in a dismissive shrug. "I'm just a woman."

"I still don't like it."

"I'll be fine." She knew he was worried and did her best to help him see this was the only way. "We don't have any real proof to connect Jerry to the blackmail except a hunch. We need a confession. Once we have something to take to the police, they can find evidence against him. He's not smart enough to have covered all his tracks."

"I don't want to leave Jonah here with only a babysitter," Liam said, a frown inching across his brow.

"I'll call Shelley," Paige offered. "I'm sure she'll be glad to have him."

Five minutes later, she ended the call to her friend who said she'd be happy to have Jonah stay with her family.

The following morning, the specially equipped pin attached to her jacket lapel, Paige called Jerry and arranged a meeting. He sounded surprised, but not alarmed, to hear from her.

When she showed up a half hour later, he greeted her genially. "Ms. Walker. Good to see you again. How can I help you?"

"It's more how we can help each other. I suppose you heard about Reva Thomas," Paige said with no preliminaries.

Jerry gave a cautious nod. "Who'd have thought it? Her being mayor and all and killing those people."

"She told Liam and me that she was being blackmailed."

"No kidding?"

"No kidding," she mimicked, her tone openly mocking. "I know what you've been doing, Jerry. Blackmailing Reva. It's too bad that the well has dried up. But I'm sure you'll find another angle to play."

He raised a brow and regarded her quizzically. "I don't know what you're talking about."

"Don't you? Reva told us all about the blackmail. She just didn't know who was behind it. It didn't take much to figure out that it was you. Don't worry. I didn't tell Liam. Or the police. Yet." She paused, letting that sink in. "We'll keep it just between the two of us. I can see a bright future for us.

"It's time you shared some of the wealth, Jerry. Consider this payment for the blackmail. Give me half of what you got from Reva and I'll keep my mouth shut."

"You're imagining things, lady."

"No. I'm smart. When Reva told us what she was being blackmailed for, I knew it had to be you."

"Still don't know what you're talking about." Though he hadn't made a move, his voice had taken on a sinister note and the corners of his mouth turned down ever so slightly.

"Okay. Try this. Sam was different after the accident. You said so yourself. Liam said he was real quiet on the way home from the game. It was easy enough to deduce that he had seen what Reva had done and had put it together. Only Sam was a good guy. He'd never consider blackmail. In the end, he told you. Maybe he didn't want the secret to die with him."

Jerry's expression smoothed out into its ordinary blandness. "Is that what you think happened? You don't have any proof."

"I think I can make a good case if I go to the police. Once they know where to look, they'll find the proof. You're sneaky, Jerry, but you're not all that smart."

"You're really good at putting things together." He

pulled a gun from behind his back and aimed it at her. "Too bad it's gonna cost you." He gestured with the gun. "Toss your phone and the weapon under your jacket over here."

She did as he instructed. He kicked the gun away, then stepped on the phone, smashing it into pieces.

"When you called this morning, I had a feeling you might have put things together. It doesn't surprise me, you being super smart and all."

"What are you planning to do?"

He looked surprised. "Kill you, of course."

"Just like that? Of course, you've already caused the deaths of three people. What's another one?"

Jerry looked affronted. "Hey, I didn't kill those people. That's on Reva."

"You started it when you sent the first blackmail demand. Didn't you care what would happen?"

"That's a lie. She started it when she drugged Old Goat Pope's water fifteen years ago. I just made it work for me. Too bad Sam didn't tell me what she'd done way back then. I could have milked this thing for years. Come to think of it, though, she wouldn't have had any dough back then, so I guess it worked out okay." Anger twisted his features into an ugly scowl. "I had a good thing going, and then you and that boyfriend of yours put an end to it."

"Do you expect us to apologize for stopping a murderer?"

"You could have minded your own business. You didn't have to get involved."

"You're as bad as she is." *Keep him talking. Give Liam time to get in position.*

"I don't remember blackmail being part of the Big Ten." At her blank look, he said, "You know, the commandments that they're always preaching about in church."

"You went to church?"

"Only because my ma made me. Like I said, blackmail's not one of them."

She stared at him incredulously. "That's your excuse? That blackmail isn't listed in the Ten Commandments? Your blackmail caused three deaths. I think that makes the Big Ten, as you call them."

"I know what you're doing. You're stalling, waiting for McKenzie to show up. Guess you and me have the same thought. I can hardly wait." Glee lit his eyes.

The sly expression on his face had her tensing.

"Now we got us some things to do. Want to have you all nice and ready for when that white knight of yours shows up." Using his weapon, he pointed to a chair. "Sit down." He produced a roll of duct tape and started wrapping her wrists to the arms of the chair, then bound her ankles together. "We'll just wait for McKenzie to come and then we'll have ourselves a nice little going-away party. Get it? You and your boyfriend are going away. Forever."

She got it. "I thought you didn't hold with killing."

"I never said that. I just said that I didn't kill the folks who already died."

"Your distinction is a fine one." Her sarcasm appeared wasted on him, for he grinned.

"You don't want to kill Liam. He was Sam's friend."

"You think that matters to me?"

"It should."

"Why should I care about Sam's friend when I could barely tolerate my brother? He was always being held up to me as what I could be if I only tried. I was a screwup. I was never allowed to forget that."

"And that means you should kill his friend?"

Smug added mean to the smirk. "No. It means I don't care that I have to kill his friend and you."

Paige stared in shock at the casual attitude toward life. "I'm sorry."

"Are you?"

"I'm sorry for anyone who regards life so cheaply."

"You're a fine one to talk. I did some digging on you. Didn't you get your fiancé killed when you were with the ATF?"

His words sucker punched her. Hadn't she said the same thing to herself? Hearing them uttered by someone else intensified her guilt.

"Nothing to say for yourself?" The derisive laugh that followed poured acid on the open wound.

"You're despicable."

He snickered. "Better that than dead." He checked the bindings around her wrists and ankles. "Make yourself comfortable while we wait."

"Tell me how you came up with the idea of blackmail."

"He didn't." A voice from behind caused her to start.

She recognized the voice. That was a twist she hadn't counted on, though it made sense now. Pieces clicked into place. The same class picture she'd seen at the Hawkins's home sat on the mantel in the Newley living room. If only she'd made the connection earlier.

He made a half circle around the chair and faced her, a .38 tucked in the waistband of his jeans.

"Calvin Pope Jr. Or do you go by Hawkins like your mother?"

"It's still Pope." His face drew into taut lines. "I can't stomach that woman. The last thing I wanted was to change my name with her, though I pretended to go along with it."

Paige recalled Liam wondering if Cal and his mother had been working in tandem. Liam had one part of the partnership right but had been off base in the other.

Cal and Jerry. It made sense. Two men the same age, both feeling that life had given them a raw deal.

She looked from one to the other. "You two were in it together."

"Sure we were," Jerry said. "We were in the same class until Cal's ma up and moved them out of town. We stayed in touch off and on. When he read about Sam dying, he came to the funeral. He stayed on after everyone left. We got to talking, and I told him what Sam told me. Cal here's got a real talent for knowing how to use information.

"It was him who came up with the idea of getting you and McKenzie out to that old trailer. It would have worked, too, if you hadn't gotten out at the last minute."

"Pretty neat trick," Paige said. "Too bad we survived."

"I knew you and McKenzie were trouble soon as you paid that visit to Ma," Cal said. "I'd hoped that the Thomas woman would take care of you, but she failed. She couldn't do anything right."

"Why?" Paige asked, directing the question to Cal. "Why blackmail Reva? Sure, you and Jerry got some money, but divided two ways, it's not that much, not worth going to jail for."

"The money was all right, but when I learned what she'd done to my pa, what she'd done to my family, I wanted payback. You saw how my ma is. I have to live with that day after day and take care of her. Things weren't good at home before the accident, but they got bad afterward. Real bad, especially after my old man left. All because some spoiled brat decided to play a trick. Reva Thomas needed to be taken down a peg, and I knew just how to do it."

Revenge.

Paige had dismissed the idea of revenge being the motive behind the killings. From the start, though, Liam had maintained that revenge was involved. He'd been right, but he'd missed the true reason for it.

"I helped Jerry figure out how we could make what Reva had done work for us," Cal said. "From there, it was simple enough to send the blackmail notes. She was willing to pay through the nose to avoid having her secret come out."

Cal was obviously the brains of the partnership, causing fear to take root in Paige's heart. Liam was going to show up, expecting he'd have only Jerry to contend with. Cal Pope presented a much more able opponent. She reminded herself that Liam was more than a match for these two amateurs, but the element of surprise worked in their favor.

She had to free herself. Now.

She twisted her hands, struggling to find some give in her bindings, but Jerry had taken pleasure in making them as tight as possible. Her hands and ankles were growing numb as the circulation was all but cut off.

"Please, I can't feel my hands," she said, injecting tears into her voice. *Disarm them. Make them see you as helpless.*

Jerry smirked. "Not going to work, lady. You might as well stop trying to free yourself. Think I don't know what you're doing? I might not be as smart as Cal here, but I know a con when I hear it."

She stopped struggling against the bindings. Jerry pulled out his cell, checked the time. "Your boyfriend's late."

"He's not coming. I told you." She injected a note of indifference in her voice. "This was my play. Why should I split the money with him?"

"Oh, I think he'll come all right," Cal said. "I saw how he looked at you when you visited my ma. You two ruined a good deal for Jerry and me. Reva would have kept paying. She would have had to if she wanted to keep that fancy life of hers, but you and your boyfriend put an end to that."

"She murdered three people because of the two of you."

Cal's mouth stretched in an ugly sneer. "No skin off my nose."

She glared at the men. "Don't either of you feel any regret at all for what you did?"

"I got a bunch of money," Jerry said. "That's the best feeling in the world. All my life, I had to do without. Now I have a nest egg. Once I take care of you and your boyfriend, I'm home free." He gave a high-pitched giggle, the sound obscene coming from a grown man. "Except I won't be at home." Another giggle. "I figure to do some traveling. You know, hobnob with the rich and famous."

"How far do you think that money is going to take you?"

"Far enough. I don't really care as long as it's away from this Podunk town."

"You could have gotten a job, done something with your life."

His eyes shifted away from hers, then came back to pierce her with stinging hate. "I got better things to do than work some stupid job."

At that moment, Liam burst through the kitchen door. He caught Jerry shoulder-to-chest and gave him a hard bump. Liam then feinted right and slid in behind his opponent and thumped him hard in the back so that Jerry fell to the floor.

"I was counting on you showing up," Cal said as casually as though he were talking about the weather. "You're so predictable. Once a hero, always a hero. Too bad we have to kill you." He held his weapon against Paige's temple. "Drop your gun or your girlfriend's toast."

Liam did as directed.

"You're so sure of yourself," Cal taunted. "You could have stopped looking for the blackmailer, but you didn't. This is on your head."

Out of the corner of his eye, Liam saw Jerry start to get up and jerked his elbow back and upward, catching Jerry in the jaw and sending him sprawling once more. Liam snatched his weapon from the floor.

Jerry stared up, eyes wide in disbelief. "You weren't supposed to do that." He sounded like a child, protesting the unfairness of an action.

Cal looked at his partner in disgust. "You always were a whiner, Jerry."

In the confusion, Liam kicked the gun from Cal's hand and slammed him to the floor, knocking him unconscious. He tied up Jerry, then undid Paige's bindings and helped her up. When she stumbled, he caught her and eased her back down in the chair. "Easy."

"Sorry. Guess my circulation is a little off."

"Stay right here. I'm going to check on him."

Blood gushed from Jerry's mouth. Liam had little desire to help this man who had caused so much pain, but he stooped to hand Jerry a handkerchief to staunch the bleeding from his lost teeth. "That should hold you for a while."

"It wasn't supposed to go down this way." The wail in Jerry's voice caused Liam to regard him with disgust.

"Your brother was one of the finest men I ever knew. What happened to you?"

But Jerry was too busy blubbering. "You hurt me." The incredulous words delivered in a childish tone would have been funny if the situation weren't so tragic.

"Consider yourself fortunate that I didn't kill you." Liam turned back to Paige. "Are you all right?"

"I am now."

Liam sent a contemptuous look in Jerry's direction.

Focused on Liam, Paige didn't see that Cal had gotten to his knees and had pulled a knife from the back of his waistband. When he plunged it into Liam's left side, she screamed and delivered a chopping blow to Cal's windpipe.

But she was too late.

FIFTEEN

Pain was a bright sphere blossoming in Liam's side. He must have blanked out for a moment, because the next thing he was aware of was hands going through his pockets.

Why was someone going through his pockets? Did he ask the question aloud? He must have said something, for a familiar yet frantic voice said, "I'm looking for your phone. Jerry took mine."

Paige's voice.

He held on to it.

"Back pocket." Did he get out the words? With his mind floating, he wasn't certain.

More talking, though he was pretty sure it wasn't to him. He let the words float over him. If he concentrated too hard, the pain returned. With a vengeance.

"I called 911. Help will be here any moment." Paige's voice again.

Help? Yes, he needed help. He couldn't catch his breath, couldn't speak. He tried, but even to his own ears, the words sounded like gibberish.

"P-Paige."

"I'm here. Right here. Don't try to talk."

"You…all right?"

"I'm fine. Thanks to you. Cal pulled a knife from his waistband. I should have been watching, should have…"

He tried to focus, but her voice faded in and out. Or maybe it was he who was fading in and out. He couldn't tell.

"I can't remove the knife, Liam. It has to stay there." Tears coated her voice, turning it murky in his mind.

Still, he did his best to listen. Paige was all right. That was what mattered.

"D-don't cry."

"I'll cry if I want to."

That was his Paige. Fierce. Feisty. And no quarter given.

Footsteps. Voices. Noises he couldn't identify. And always that pop of pain that refused to go away. He regained consciousness enough to note the arrival of the police and EMTs.

"Liam." Paige's voice again. He concentrated on that. "Help's here. It will be all right." But the sob in her voice negated her words.

Don't cry, he wanted to tell her.

A voice he recognized. Reineke's. There was no mistaking the Boston accent.

"Let's turn him over." A second voice. Firm. Reassuring.

Liam struggled to say that he didn't want to move, didn't want hands probing where the pain was radiating in ever bigger circles.

"You're going to be okay."

But the words failed to register. A prick in the arm startled him. Why was someone sticking something sharp in his arm when he was already hurting more than he'd ever hurt in his life? He wanted to protest but found the effort too much.

More voices. One insistent. Another calm. Why were they arguing when he just wanted to sleep? He tried to tell them to be quiet, but once again the words came out as gibberish.

Darkness beckoned, the oblivion of it welcoming. He fought against it, though he wasn't sure why. Hadn't he just told the voices that he wanted to sleep? Nothing made sense, least of all the images in his mind that kept shifting from one scene to another. The more he tried to force his mind to work, the greater the pain grew. He struggled against the fog of semiconsciousness.

"I'm going with him." Paige again.

He recognized that tone. It was the one she used when she was convinced she was right and wasn't going to back down no matter what. *Good for you*, he wanted to say, though he didn't know for what he was congratulating her.

Strong hands rolled him onto something. A cot? No, they wouldn't be putting him onto a cot. Then he was being carried. He was fairly certain of that. Where were they taking him? Somewhere the pain couldn't reach him, he hoped.

Footsteps sounded, a rhythmic pace that lulled him into a state of near-sleep. He settled into it, thankful that the pain seemed to have subsided. If he could have, he'd have wept in gratitude. But even that required too much effort.

"I'm going with him, so make room."

Paige would get her way. On that, he drifted off.

Before she climbed into the ambulance, Paige spared a moment to identify Jerry and Cal to Detective Reineke. "Jerry Newley and Calvin Pope. They were in on the blackmail together, set the whole thing in motion. It's because of them that three people are dead."

Reineke nodded. "We'll take care of them. You take care of your man. I'll catch up with you later."

Intent on going with Liam, she didn't bother to answer. She gave no heed to the EMTs who were doing their best to force her out of the ambulance. She was going to accompany Liam to the hospital, and that was that.

"I'm here," she said, "and I'm not going anywhere."

She supposed that the aggressive tilt of her chin must have convinced the two EMTs who had climbed in the back of the ambulance that she meant business, because they shrugged at each other and relented.

"Stay out of the way," one said, "and if we say move, you move. Got it?"

"Got it."

She knelt by the gurney where Liam lay. Pale. So very pale. The knife had gone in under his left arm, close, too close, to his heart. Blood no longer gushed from the wound, but it had been gushing earlier, draining Liam of his life force.

Please don't let him die. Please don't let him die. The words chanted through her mind. She'd loved two men in her life. Ethan was the first. And now Liam.

She couldn't lose him. Not now. Not when she was beginning to think they had a future, a life together.

How had she not seen Cal go for his knife? She doubted she'd ever be able to forgive herself for that. She should have been watching.

He'd had it on him all the time, waiting for the right moment. The law would take care of him, but she couldn't bring herself to care about that right now.

"They'll be waiting for us," the first EMT said. "We just have to get him there."

"Alive," the other muttered under his breath.

Paige prayed as she'd never prayed before. The silently uttered words repeated in her mind, a litany of begging and pleading with the Lord for His tender mercies.

When the ambulance screeched to a stop, the doors were flung open. Attendants rushed Liam inside and down a narrow hallway.

She tried to follow but was stopped.

"No farther," a nurse in green scrubs said. "We've got him now." He looked her over. "If you don't mind my saying so, maybe you want to clean up a bit."

She looked down at her hands, saw the blood coating them. Some of it had dried to a rusty stain, but fresher blood was still sticky to the touch.

"Thank you."

She found a restroom and washed her hands until the water ran clear and her skin was raw. She did her best to wash the blood from her shirt, but it was a lost cause. In the end, she took it off and threw it in the trash. The pink T-shirt she wore underneath would have to do.

When she found the waiting room, she forced herself to do what had to be done. Using Liam's phone, she called his parents, told them what happened, promised to keep them informed as they made the drive from Savannah. She then called Shelley and let her know what had gone down.

After assuring Shelley that she was all right, Paige asked about Jonah.

"He's fine. Playing with Tommy and Chloe. They're all running through the house with the dog chasing them."

After they ended the call, Paige paced the length of the waiting room. The repeated steps did little to settle her racing thoughts. And then it came to her. Every hospital had a chapel, and she sought it out. There, she poured out her heart to the Lord, ending with a simple "Amen." She remained on her knees for long minutes before finally returning to the waiting room and resuming her pacing. When the doctor appeared, she ran to him.

"You're here for Liam McKenzie?" the doctor, a dark-haired woman with kind eyes, asked.

Paige nodded. "Yes. Please. Tell me."

"I'm Dr. Nouri. Your friend's going to be okay. The knife didn't nick his lung, though it came close. He'll stay here for a few days, then he can recuperate at home."

"Thank you, Doctor. Thank you." *Liam is going to be all right. Thank You, Lord.*

"He's young and strong, a point in his favor, but I can't emphasize enough that he needs rest."

Liam is going to be all right. Paige repeated the words in her mind, a litany of gratitude and prayer. If she said them enough, even if uttered silently, maybe the lump in her throat would dissolve and she could breathe again. "Can I see him?"

"Just for a minute. Don't be alarmed by how he looks. He's lost a lot of blood and has over thirty stitches in his side."

Paige made a hurried call to Liam's parents to reassure them that their son would be all right and that she'd made arrangements for Jonah. Grateful she'd cleaned up a bit, she made her way to Liam's room.

Hooked up to beeping machines by a variety of tubes, Liam looked nearly as colorless as the institutional white walls. The energy and determination that were so much a part of him were absent. Tears leaked from her eyes to trickle down her cheeks.

"Liam," she whispered. "I'm here."

He stirred but didn't wake. She lifted his hand, gave

it a gentle squeeze. Was it her imagination or did he return the pressure?

A nurse appeared, her smile understanding, her words firm. "I'm sorry, but you'll have to leave now. Doctor's orders."

"Of course."

Paige returned to the waiting room. When a middle-aged couple rushed in, the man bearing a striking resemblance to Liam and the woman a petite brunette at his side, Paige hurried to them. "Mr. and Mrs. McKenzie?"

"Yes." The man offered his hand. "And you'd be the one who called us."

"That's right. Paige Walker."

"We can't thank you enough," the woman said. "Have you seen our boy?"

"Yes, but only for a minute. He's resting right now. The doctor says it will be a couple of days before he can leave the hospital."

"As long as he'll be all right, we can handle the rest," Mrs. McKenzie said. "We've already decided that we'll take turns staying here so someone's with him all the time."

"I'd like to be included in that, if you'll let me."

Liam's father rested a large hand on her shoulder. "Of course you can. I have a feeling that you're important to our boy."

She didn't answer that. How could she when she didn't know how things stood between her and Liam? Liam's mother nodded as though settling something important. "We're going to get along just fine." Mrs. McKenzie took Paige's hand and led her to a seat. "You look like a strong wind could knock you right over. And no wonder, with all that you've been through. You rest right here while Angus sees to matters. He's good at that."

Though Paige topped the older woman by a good five inches, she felt like a child being put to bed, but she couldn't deny that the idea of rest sounded good.

"Maybe for a minute," she murmured. She needed a minute. Just one minute to process the fact that Liam was going to be all right.

But a minute turned into a few minutes, which turned into an hour. When Paige woke, it was to find Shelley sitting beside her.

"Hi, sleepyhead."

"Mr. and Mrs. McKenzie...where are they?"

"They're visiting Liam. Before you ask, Jonah's with Caleb and the kids. When I left, he looked to be having the time of his life running through the house with the dog chasing after him. I figured you weren't going to leave any time soon, so I stopped by your place and picked up some clean clothes."

"Thank you," Paige said with fervent feeling, thinking how glad she'd be to get out of the clothes she currently had on.

Hospital noises went on around them, but Paige scarcely noticed. She was too busy worrying over how Liam was doing.

Shelley reached for Paige's hand, gave it a comforting squeeze. "I'd ask how you are, but since the last time I saw you, you've been kidnapped, used as bait and then watched Liam get stabbed. Even though I brought you clothes, I'd suggest you go home, get some rest and then come back."

"I can't. I told Liam's parents that I'd take a turn sitting with him."

Another hand squeeze. "It's you I'm worried about right now. Are you going to be all right?"

"As long as Liam's going to be all right, I'm okay. In fact, I'm better than okay."

Shelley gave her a shrewd stare. "So it's like that, is it?"

"It's like that," Paige said and leveled a steady gaze at her friend.

"Then I'm happy for you."

Paige smiled for the first time in what felt like forever. "I'm pretty happy for me, too." Then her smile faded. "I don't know what Liam feels."

"Judging from the way he looks at you, he has feelings for you."

"But are they the real thing?"

"That's not my place to answer." Shelley stood. "C'mon. Let's get you cleaned up. Those clothes you're wearing look like they should be burned." She wrinkled her nose. "Smell like it, too."

Paige noticed how rank she smelled and grimaced.

After performing what cleaning she could and changing clothes in the restroom, she felt immeasurably better. In the waiting room once more, she found Liam's parents talking with Shelley.

"I was telling Shelley that we can't thank her enough for taking care of our Jonah," Liam's mother said. "One of us will pick him up and take him to Liam's house when we get our shifts here arranged." She turned an understanding gaze on Paige. "You can go back now. He woke up for a few minutes, asked for you."

"Thank you." Paige sent Shelley a grateful smile. "And thank you. I don't know what I'd have done without you."

She walked down the hallway to Liam's room and saw that he'd fallen back to sleep. Content just to be near him and to absorb the fact that he was all right, she brought a chair closer to his bed and watched as he slept.

Mindful that she needed to trade off time sitting with him with his parents, she reluctantly returned to the waiting room and found Detective Reineke there.

"Ms. Walker. You're looking a sight better than the last time I saw you."

"Thank you. You've met Mr. McKenzie's parents?"

"We've introduced ourselves. If you'll excuse us," he said to Liam's parents, "Ms. Walker and I need to talk."

Relieved that he had the tact not to talk in front of them, Paige followed him to an empty grouping of chairs.

The detective opened a small notebook. "We interviewed Jerry Newley. I guess he figured he wouldn't get anywhere with lying, seeing as you and Mr. McKenzie were right there and can testify against him. He spilled the whole thing, starting with the first blackmail note up to holding you hostage. You'll have to come in and make a statement at some point, but that can wait."

"Thank you."

"You put yourself in a great deal of danger." The tone was reproving but not unkind. Maybe she and the detective were going to be friends after all.

"I know."

"I'm glad you're all right and that your man is going to be all right, too." After a few questions, he took his leave, but Paige paid scant attention. She was too busy pondering his words. *Your man.*

Dark dreams chased him.

Liam tried to outrun them, to hide from their ruthless pursuit, but they caught up with him. Blackness swirled around him as he careened through unchartered territory, leaving him disoriented and confused as he searched. Even more disturbing was the idea that he didn't know for whom or what he was looking.

Then it came to him. Paige was missing. He had to find her, had to rescue her from the cruel forces that had carried her away. She was in danger. How could he have forgotten? Guilt for his careless memory lashed his soul with stinging stripes.

He pushed his way through the shadows, seeking any hint of light to point the way. Why couldn't he see the course that would take him to Paige? Why was he so lost? The path was there. All he had to do was find it.

But he wasn't given the light he so desperately needed and so continued to wander in the darkness, a harsh wilderness where any moment a shadow could shift into an enemy.

Pain was a constant companion, a pitiless master that drained him of all energy and will. Had he been injured? He couldn't remember. The pain was playing tricks on his mind, but the thought that Paige needed him pushed him forward. Jumbled memories with Jerry and Cal Jr. found their way into the nightmares.

At one point, he thought he called out Paige's name.

"I'm here. Liam, I'm right here beside you."

Did he imagine the words? He couldn't tell. He tried to shake his head, to clear it of the fogginess that had taken up residence there. He wanted to ask her something but couldn't put words to the question.

Apparently reading his mind, she said, "The police have Jerry and Cal Jr. in custody. They'll be going away for a very long time."

He tried to answer but couldn't make his tongue work. He couldn't move. Something was holding him back.

Ropes…no, tubes, he thought. He was in a hospital. When it came to him, he wondered why it had taken him so long to figure it out.

"Liam, it's going to be all right."

That voice again. He calmed. "Paige?"

"Yes."

"'Kay?" His voice slurred the word into a single syllable.

"I'm okay. Go back to sleep."

That sounded like a fine idea.

When he woke again, it was to find sun streaming through the windows and his parents at his side. Had they been there all night? No, Paige had been there. At least he thought she had.

His parents looked tired, and he read the worry in their eyes. "H-hey."

The smile his mother gave him was the one he'd always thought of as her my-boy-is-okay-but-I-still-worry-about-him smile. He supposed it'd be the same for him and Jonah no matter how old his own boy grew to be.

"How are you feeling, son?" his father asked.

Liam did a quick inventory. "Like I got stabbed with a really big knife, but I'm going to live anyway."

The deep rumble of laughter from his father reassured him that everything was going to be okay.

"Jonah?" he asked.

"Paige told us that she'd arranged for him to stay with her friend Shelley until we can pick him up."

"We like Paige," his mother said. "She's very pretty. More, she's kind and thoughtful. And smart. I can see why she's special to you."

"She's not…" Liam broke off what he'd been about

to say. Paige was special to him. There was no sense in denying it.

When he drifted off once more, he wondered if he was special to Paige, as well.

Later on, she said that there was a time—

It had said, "I am delighted, apparently, to see
you. It seemed likely—"

SIXTEEN

Boy and puppy sounds filled the room.

A trip to the animal shelter had resulted in bringing
home a Heinz 57 mix whose bright eyes and inquisitive
expression had immediately caught Jonah's heart and
melted Liam's own. Jonah had inexplicably named him
Ralph, so Ralph it was.

"Daddy, can Ralph and I play outside?" Jonah asked.
"In the backyard."

The backyard was enclosed with what Liam hoped
was puppy-proof fencing, a new installment and a must,
the shelter director had explained, to keep Ralph from
digging under an ordinary fence not meant to stand up
to a puppy's inquisitive nature.

Squeals and barks moved from indoors to out.

Liam had been home for two weeks. He could move
without hurting and was almost back to normal. Life had
also returned to normal. Only he didn't know what normal was. Did it include Paige?

When his parents had returned to their home, she had
come over nearly every day that first week to help with
Jonah and, despite Liam's protests, do some housework.
He realized he *wanted* her in his life. Permanently.

The trick was to convince her that they belonged together. Forever.

With Jonah and Ralph in the backyard playing, the house was quiet. He had no doubt that would not last for long. At his desk, Liam could watch boy and dog and work on a new software design at the same time.

Within a few minutes, though, he pushed his laptop away and rolled his shoulders. Work held little appeal as thoughts of Paige occupied his mind. She filled the empty parts of him, the parts he hadn't known needed filling. He worked to find the right word to describe how he felt with her and came up with *whole*.

Whole. Complete. Finished.

With Paige, he was the man he was meant to be. Up until her, Jonah had been his life. And would continue to be. No one would change that. But she brought a new level of meaning to his life, a new way of seeing what had once been unclear. With his faith restored, he could work on his inner self.

"Thank You, Lord." The words came naturally, a sweet confirmation that he had indeed regained his belief in the Lord and His love.

"Daddy, who are you talking to?" Jonah asked.

Somehow Jonah and Ralph had come inside without Liam being aware of it. He shook himself out of his musings and smiled at his son. "I was thanking the Lord for being part of our lives."

Jonah considered. "That's good. I like going to church."

That was another change they'd recently made. Father and son had started attending church. One Sunday, Paige had joined them. It had been good, sitting in the reverent service with her on one side and Jonah on the other.

"I think Ralph is hungry."

Ralph, it appeared, was always hungry.

"I'm hungry, too," Jonah added.

"Okay, let's get you boys something to eat. But first," Liam added with a rueful look at Jonah's hands and Ralph's feet, "the two of you need to get cleaned up.

"You wash your hands, and I'll take care of Ralph."

With a great deal of giggling on Jonah's part and resistance on Ralph's, the two boys were cleaned up and ready for a snack. Jonah had some cookies, courtesy of a care package from his grandma, while Ralph was given kibble.

"Can Ralph have a cookie?" Jonah asked. "He told me that he liked chocolate chip cookies."

Liam raised a brow. "He did, did he?"

Jonah nodded solemnly.

"Chocolate's not good for dogs," Liam said, equally solemnly. "Let's stick with kibble. We don't want to make Ralph sick, do we?"

Jonah gave a vigorous shake of his head. "No! I'm sorry, Ralph," he said to the puppy, who looked first at the son and then the father, "but you can't have cookies."

Ralph favored them with what could only be described as a reproach, then returned to eating his puppy chow.

"I can't wait to show Ralph to Grandma and Grandpa," Jonah said between bites. "Do you think they'll like him?"

Liam smiled. "I'm sure your grandparents will love Ralph." Because they loved Jonah.

"Can Ralph sleep with me tonight?"

That had been a sticking point. Liam had wanted to kennel-train Ralph, who had mourned woefully at being separated from Jonah.

"What if we compromise and Ralph sleeps in his kennel in your bedroom?"

Jonah thought about it. "Can we put the kennel on my bed?"

Liam didn't have the heart to refuse. "The kennel can go on your bed. You realize, don't you, that as Ralph gets bigger, his kennel will also get bigger?"

Another period of thought on Jonah's part followed. "I guess I'll need a bigger bed."

His son's unassailable logic had Liam chuckling to himself. "I guess you will." How could he argue when both boy and dog looked at him with beseeching expressions?

"There's enough time for you and Ralph to play outside again before we get dinner started," Liam said.

"Okay." With a swipe of his mouth to brush away cookie crumbs and a whoop of joy, Jonah took off, Ralph at his heels. The ensuing racket reached outside, and Liam could only imagine the calls from irate neighbors he was bound to receive. Obedience school for Ralph was next on the list.

When the doorbell rang, Liam went to answer it, wondering if it was a complaining neighbor already.

It wasn't a neighbor.

Paige stood on his front porch, her face as bright and cheerful as the armful of yellow tulips she held.

She handed the flowers to him. "I thought your house needed some flowers," she said.

She was right. The house, his home, needed color and the scent of fresh flowers. It needed her. Just as he did.

"Thank you." He carried the flowers to the kitchen and put them in the only thing he could find—a water pitcher. As much as he'd tried to make the house a home, it didn't run to such things as vases.

"Perfect," she said and came to stand beside him.

He took her hand in his and brought her to the sofa. "We need to talk."

Her gaze questioning, she nodded.

Liam struggled for what to say. He settled on telling her about adding a new member to the family. "Jonah has been wanting a dog forever. After…everything, it seemed the right time."

He filled the time talking about the puppy's antics. "Yesterday he got his head caught in the banister railing. I almost had to take it apart to free him."

She smiled. "He must have been annoyed."

"*I* was the one who was annoyed," he said with mock gruffness.

"Liam, is Ralph getting his head caught in a banister really what you wanted to talk to me about?" she asked with gentle humor.

"Uh…no. I was trying to set the atmosphere."

"You were trying to set the atmosphere to talk about Ralph?" A teasing note crept into her words.

"No," he said more firmly and was reminded of all the reasons he loved her. More important than her beauty and intelligence, she had so much humor and compassion and total lack of selfishness that she took his breath away. Even with all the losses she'd endured in life, she was filled with hope and faith and had dedicated her life to helping others, to seeking justice.

"I was trying to set the atmosphere to tell you that I love you and want you in my life. I want to make a home with Jonah, Ralph and you. That wasn't how I planned on saying it." He huffed out an annoyed-at-himself breath. "I love you, Paige."

"I love you, too."

"One thing. I'm turning my company over to the vice

president to manage. I've been offered a job with the US Marshals. I've decided to take it."

"Oh?"

If ever a single syllable held caution, it was this.

He chose his next words with care. "I was hoping you'd be happy for me." He added a smile, hoping he'd get one in return.

She freed her hands from his. "Is that what you want? To join the marshals?"

His buoyant mood of only moments ago took a puncture wound. He prayed it wasn't fatal.

"Being with you, working on the case, reminded me of how much I liked my work when I was with the CID."

The army's Criminal Investigative Division was one of the world's elite law enforcement agencies. "I want to make a difference. The Marshals Service has been after me for some time. The head honcho seems to think my computer skills will come in handy."

"So you'd be riding a desk?"

"Well, that and other things." Now it was his turn to be cautious.

Paige circled the room, came back to face him. "If this is what you want, then I'm happy for you. I really am."

The *but* hung so loudly in the air that he could all but see it forming a barrier between them. "But?" He reached up to cup her jaw and felt the resistance there. More than resistance, though, was distance.

She took a step backward. Another. The actual distance involved was small, but the emotional chasm it created was deep enough to drown in. "But I don't know if I can be a part of it. I don't know if I *want* to be part of it."

All at once, the distance grew and loomed in front of him, a void filled with unanswered questions, unbroken silences.

"I don't understand." That was the truth. He didn't understand. "You just said you loved me."

"I do." She paused, one of those pauses that made you wonder if it would last forever. "You almost died a couple of weeks ago. I was there with you, praying with everything I had. Begging the Lord to keep you alive."

"I know." Her prayers had likely saved his life. But even before that, he'd recognized that he needed the Lord in his life.

"What do your parents think?"

"About what you'd expect. They'd feel better if I stayed with the software company, but they want me to be happy."

"How about safe? Do they want you to be safe, too?" Her voice took on an accusing note. Apparently she heard it as well for she took a deep breath. "Of course they do. I saw how much they love you."

"They know I'm not going to do anything foolish." This wasn't going the way he'd planned.

"You almost died."

"You said that."

"I lost Ethan." Her voice caught, and she turned away.

He placed his hands on her shoulders, gently turned her around. When she avoided his gaze, he put a finger beneath her chin and lifted it so that their eyes met. His heart bumped up to his throat, and he yearned to take away all the pain harbored inside her. He recognized it as pain because he had experienced the same sense of loss, of grief.

She lifted her gaze. "Sometimes I think I'm over the heartache of his dying, but then something happens. A memory trigger, I call it. And it all floods back. The grief, the bewilderment, the wondering why." She brushed at the tears that ran down her cheeks. "Then there're the questions. Could I have stopped it? If I'd been better at my job, could I have stopped the lowlife who took that shot?"

"Paige." He wanted to wipe away the tears. To hold her and promise nothing would ever hurt her again. But such thoughts were futile, and so he held his tongue. The temptation was strong to take her in his arms, but this wasn't the time. Or the place. "You're smart enough to know that none of that is true. I know you—I know you did everything you could to save Ethan. It isn't in you to do less."

"How can you know? I don't even know." She sounded lost, so unlike her usual confident self. "The past has a way of reinventing itself," she said. "Just when you think you've made peace with it, think you're over it, something happens and you realize you're not over it at all."

"I know. But I'm not Ethan." By force of will, he refrained from shouting the words, even when he'd wanted to roar them, such was his frustration. He took her hands in his once more and gentled his voice. "I survived two tours in Afghanistan. I think I can handle being a marshal here in the States."

"Don't you dare downplay it." The words cracked through the air, an indictment of his attempt to do exactly that—downplay it. "I've worked with marshals in the past. They handle WITSEC. They also escort high-value prisoners. It's not a day in the park."

"No, it's not. But I need it. After everything we've been through, I thought you'd understand. You put your life on the line. I've seen you do it." It would be all right, he told himself. She just needed time to get used to it.

Her voice turned defensive. "That's not typical for me. I usually sit behind a desk playing geek."

"Geek is good, and I've done it for a number of years.

Maybe I will again. But right now I want more. I need more. Can't you understand?" He heard the pleading in the words. Since when did he beg?

"No, I don't understand at all. What about Jonah?"

"Jonah doesn't care what I do, only that I love him."

"And if something happens to you? What then?" Accusation rang in her words, and he found himself reacting to it.

"It won't." The snap in his voice caused him to pull back, to try to understand where she was coming from. "It won't."

"I can't be with another man who puts himself in harm's way."

"I'm not Ethan." He kept his tone even, though he was beginning to resent being compared to a dead man. In an attempt to hold on to his temper, he drew in a sharp breath.

There was that distance again. And with it, he feared, an impenetrable wall between them. Paige wanted a guarantee that he wouldn't be hurt, and he couldn't, in all honesty, give that to her.

"You want to deny what we have because you can't see past your fears." Now he was the one who sounded accusing.

"That's not fair. I love you. That's not going to change. But I can't lose you like that. I can't go through that again. I *won't* go through it again."

"Who says you're going to lose me? Why can't you apply that faith of yours to me, to know that I won't take any unnecessary risks, that I will always come home to you and Jonah?"

She shook her head. "I'm sorry. Sorrier than I can say. I can't be the woman you need." Tears filled her eyes.

Once more, he longed to brush them away, but he kept

his hands at his sides. It took everything he had to not reach for her. "Is that it?"

In answer, she walked away.

Two weeks had passed since Paige had walked out of Liam's house. And out of his life. A dozen times, two dozen times, she'd started to call him and tell him that she loved him no matter what, but she realized she'd be losing herself if she gave in to that temptation.

S&J headquarters was busy today, with clients and operatives coming and going. She managed to slip past Shelley's office, made her way to her own, and, gratefully, closed the door. Resolutely, she started on the paperwork she'd promised herself she'd get to when she had time.

Well, she had time right now. Lots of time.

She finished the report on Liam's case, the report she'd found one excuse after another not to complete. After copying it to both Shelley and Jake, she told herself that that chapter of her life was over. Without a new case to work on, she started backing up the files she'd neglected over the last weeks. Systematically, she went through the motions, but her mind—and her heart—were elsewhere. And would, she feared, remain so.

A pang of regret hit her as she thought of the last time she'd seen Liam. They had been so right together, in every way but one. How could she love another man whose job put him in danger?

The answer was simple—she couldn't. Couldn't give her heart to a man who could be taken away as Ethan had been.

There was only one problem with that: she *was* in love with Liam. He was strong without being dominating, tender without being weak. When she was with him, her knees turned to jelly. A half smile crossed her lips at the cliché. She supposed that was why the phrase had taken on cliché status—it was the truth.

After bringing up a favorite music app on her phone, she found a song that would drown out the sounds of her sick heart. Did hearts make noise outside of the normal beating? Apparently so. Hers was crying. Inside where it didn't show but really hurt. She could hear it. Anyone listening could hear it. She was certain of it.

When Shelley poked her head in, Paige did her best to wipe her face clean. The last thing she wanted was her friend to know that she was mooning over a man she couldn't have. However, she hadn't reckoned with Shelley's perception.

"What's wrong?" No beating around the bush for Shelley.

"Nothing."

"Liar," Shelley said softly. "You've been moping around the office for the last two weeks. I let you get away with it because I figured you'd come clean eventually, but you haven't. So, give."

Paige didn't answer directly. Instead, she asked, "How did you know that you and Caleb were right?"

"I didn't. Not at first. I don't think he did, either. But we got there. Partly because we're both stubborn and when we want something, we go for it. Partly, also, because I knew that there would never be anyone else for me. Caleb was it.

"That doesn't mean there weren't bumps along the way. There were more than enough to go around, what with adopting Tommy and making him feel part of a family. Sometimes there still are, but we navigate our way through them. Do you want to know something I learned along the way?"

She didn't wait for Paige to nod. "Life is fragile. We don't know what will come, so whenever possible, choose joy. Joy is a choice, so when it presents itself, seize it with both hands and your whole heart and hold on to it."

Paige heard the certainty in her friend's voice. "Choose joy," she repeated softly. "I like that." How far did the bounds of friendship go? Dare she ask her next question?

"Are you ever afraid that something will happen and you won't be able to…how did you put it…navigate your way through it?"

"Sometimes. But then I remember it's not just Caleb and me and the kids. We have the Lord on our side. Remembering that makes all the difference."

For all her talk of belief and faith, Paige realized she'd forgotten to take the Lord into account. He was always there, and, if she and Liam allowed Him to, He would seal His love upon them.

"You're in love with Liam, aren't you?"

Miserably, Paige nodded and shoved a fist in her mouth to quell the sob building in her chest. Realizing that she'd given herself away, she removed her fist and gave Shelley a wan smile. "How'd you guess?"

"How does he feel?"

"He said he loves me, and I believe him. But he wants something that I can't agree to. He has an offer to join the US Marshals. He's going to take it. He'd be great at it, but…"

"But you're worried that something will happen to him," Shelley guessed.

"What if I lose him? I don't think I could bear it."

"What if you don't? What if you build a wonderful life together? But if something were to happen to him, would it hurt any less if you weren't married to him? If you had to watch from afar, wanting to be there for him but knowing you couldn't because you didn't have the right?"

Paige could only stare at her friend. The simplicity of it stunned her. Of course it wouldn't hurt any less if she had no official part of Liam's life. She loved him. That didn't go away just because she didn't have a marriage certificate to prove it.

"Love is a promise," Shelley said. "It's the promise, knowing that you each want the other in your life." She hugged Paige. "I'll let you think on that."

Shelley's words remained with Paige long after her friend left. She mulled them over and was shamed by her cowardice in refusing to have the courage to share a life with Liam.

Love. Where she could lean and not lose part of herself, where he could do the same. That's what it was all about.

The other—jobs, where they lived—that could be figured out.

But love…that was the key. She loved Liam. With all her heart. It didn't make any difference whether she was married to him or not. It wouldn't change her feelings, the love she carried in her heart for him. Why had it taken her so long to figure it out?

She'd been a fool. She could only pray he'd find it in him to forgive her.

After arranging with Shelley to take the rest of the day off, Paige headed to Liam's house.

He opened the door and gazed at her quizzically.

"Hi." She winced inwardly. The greeting was totally inadequate, but it had been all she'd been able to come up with.

She was aware of time moving very, very slowly. *One*

one thousand, two one thousand, three one thousand...
How many seconds—or was it minutes—had to pass before he said something?

Finally she broke the silence. "Are you going to invite me in?"

"Uh...sure." Liam stood back. "Come on in."

"Thanks."

"I didn't expect to see you." There was longing in his eyes, and any worry that he might not have missed her as much as she missed him vanished.

"I didn't expect to be here." *Okay, Walker, you can do better than that.* "I came to apologize." That, and a lot more.

"Apologize?"

"I had no right to tell you how to run your life."

"You didn't."

"I came pretty close. I was out of line. Mostly, I was—"

The French doors opened, and Jonah and a puppy skidded inside. "Daddy, we..." His words skidded to a stop just as his feet had. "Hi, Miss Walker."

"Hi, Jonah."

"Do you want to meet my puppy? This is Ralph. Ralph, say hi to Miss Walker. She's really nice."

Ralph barked enthusiastically.

What did she say upon being introduced to a dog? "Uh...hi, Ralph."

"We just got Ralph a couple of weeks ago. He's my best friend." Jonah's freckled face bunched up in a thoughtful frown. "Well, Daddy's my best friend. And Ralph's my next best friend. You can be my friend, too. And Ralph's."

Absurdly touched, Paige smiled. "I'd like that."

"Jonah," Liam said, "why don't you and Ralph go back outside? Ms. Walker and I need to talk."

"Okay."

Jonah and his new best friend ran outside in a rush of feet and paws and what could only be described as hoots and barks of pure happiness.

With no preamble, she plunged in. "I should have trusted you when you said that you can take care of yourself. I've seen you in action. I know that you're good." She sucked in a breath. "I came to ask you to forgive me." There. It was out. She waited.

"There's nothing to forgive. You'd suffered a terrible loss, and you were dealing with it in the only way you knew how."

"I love you no matter what job you have, no matter how much I want you to be safe."

"Same goes."

Tears clogged her throat at his easy forgiveness, and Paige searched for something to say.

"Don't postpone joy," she murmured, thinking of her conversation with Shelley.

"That's an interesting observation."

"Something Shelley told me. She said we should choose joy whenever we can."

"Smart lady." He crossed the room and took her hands in his. As always, his touch sent tingles of awareness through her. "What were you going to say before that tornado blew in?"

She took a gulp of air and then forced out the words in a single breath. "I was scared. Scared of losing you."

"Why?"

"Why do you think? I love you."

A satisfied smile settled on his lips. "That's all I need to know. The rest, we can figure out."

"That's what I'm trying to say. We don't have to figure anything out. I'm okay with you joining the marshals. I'll probably worry, but I trust you to take care of yourself."

"You mean that?"

"With all my heart. The last time we talked, I forgot something very important. Or, I should say, Someone very important."

"The Lord."

Warmth filled her heart that Liam had invited the Lord into his life. Any remaining doubts she had about joining her life with Liam's disappeared. "I forgot to include Him in our relationship. If we have Him on our side, we can't lose."

"You brought Him back into my life. I can never thank you enough for that."

"He was never gone," she said softly. "You just didn't know where to look."

"Because of you, I found my belief again." His voice turned husky. "I want you in my home. In my heart. In my life. I want you and Jonah and Ralph and me to be a family, the forever kind."

Her heart, the one she thought she'd closed off, opened to joy. "That's funny. That's exactly what I want. I want together forever with you."

A frisson of excitement ruffled her senses as he gazed at her with eyes full of love.

"I'm not always easy to get along with," she warned. "I like to have my own way. I tend to think I'm right no matter what the question is. I'm—"

"Are you trying to scare me away?"

"I'm trying to warn you that we'll likely find ourselves on opposite sides of things at times."

He smiled and circled her wrist with his fingers. "I'll take the risk." He drew her to him and kissed her with so much love that her heart felt like it would burst in that instant. The kiss held the soaring sense of a man who had just escaped captivity and discovered freedom. She returned it with the same depth of feeling.

Slow and soft, spinning out this one moment in time, the kiss promised everything. She laid her hand on his heart, feeling the steadiness, the strength, the power. She wondered how she had ever endured the lonely days before Liam, knowing he would be there, beside her, with arms to hold her, a heartbeat to match the rhythm of her own. Their love was a light that would always guide her out of the dark.

She gave herself to the feelings, to him. With his arms around her, his heart beating against hers, she knew she had come home, a real home she and Liam would make together. She pulled back a few inches and traced the shape of his jaw with her fingers. Strong, like the rest of him. The steady look he gave her promised everything.

Theirs wouldn't be a life without problems—they were both too strong-willed for that—but it would be perfect because they were together.

"Will you marry me?" she asked. Since she had walked away and hadn't given him the opportunity to ask her the last time they were together, it seemed only fitting that she do the asking now.

A huge smile broke across his face. "Yes." He kissed her lightly. "Are you ready to take on a five-year-old boy and a puppy named Ralph who's going to grow into a very big dog?"

"I already love Jonah. As for the puppy, how can I not love a dog named Ralph?"

His smile infinitely tender, he fitted his hands to her waist. "I've been looking for you for a very long time. All of my life, in fact."

"And I, you. I'm here. With you. I'm not going any-where. Not today. Not ever."

"Me, either."

His lips on hers were sweet with the heady promise of today and tomorrow and all the tomorrows after that.

"I don't need a big fancy wedding. Just a simple cer-emony with Jonah and your parents and our friends. And Ralph. There's one thing I insist on, though," she said when he lifted his head. She assumed her most serious expression.

"What's that?"

"We have to have good auto insurance. Really good."

He looked perplexed, then threw back his head and laughed. "Full coverage. I promise."

She kissed him once more. "Perfect."

* * * * *

If you enjoyed Secrets from the Past, *look for these other great books from author Jane M. Choate, available now:*

Find more great reads at www.LoveInspired.com.

Dear Reader,

As I told Liam and Paige's story, I knew that I wanted to write about two strong people who were, nonetheless, broken. In Japan, broken objects are often repaired with gold. The flaw is seen as a unique piece of the object's history, which adds to its beauty.

Are we not all broken in some way? I know that I am. I am broken in many places, some more visible than others. I am broken in grief over the loss of loved ones. I am broken in pain from betrayal. I am broken in spirit when depression overcomes me.

I am broken.

And yet I know that I can be made whole once again through the atonement of the Savior. His supreme sacrifice allows me and all of us to appear once more before Him, whole, our scars repaired with the gold of His infinite love. Christ asked that our sacrifice for Him be a broken heart and a contrite spirit.

I pray that we can each find the broken parts inside us, rejoice in the refining fire of them, and then allow Jesus to heal us.

With gratitude for His love,
Jane

Lex Fielding drove, cutting down the narrow dirt path between the towering trees. Branches slapped the side of his park-ranger truck, and rocks spun beneath his wheels. All the while, words cascaded through his mind, clattering and colliding in a mass of disjointed ideas that didn't even begin to come close to what he wanted to say to Poppy. Years ago, he'd had no clue how to explain to the most incredible woman he'd ever known that he didn't think he was ready to get married and have a family. He might not have even had the guts to tell her all his doubts, if she hadn't called him out on it after he'd left a really unfortunate and accidental pocket-dial message on Poppy's voice mail admitting he wasn't ready to get married.

Something about being around Poppy had always made him feel like a better man than he had any right being. Even standing beside her made him feel an inch taller.

He just hadn't thought he'd been cut out to be anyone's husband. Something he'd then proved a couple of years later by marrying the wrong woman and surviving a couple of unhappy years together before she'd tragically died in a car crash.

He heard the chaos ahead before he could even see it through the thick forest. A dog was barking furiously, voices were shouting, and above it all was a loud and relentless banging sound, like something was trying to break down one of the cabins from the inside.

He whispered a prayer and asked God for wisdom. Hadn't been big on prayer outside of church on Sundays back when he'd been planning on marrying Poppy. But ever since Danny had been born, he'd been relying on it more and more to get through the day.

Then the trees parted, just in time for him to see the two figures directly in front of him dragging something across the road. His heart stopped.

Not something. *Someone.*

They had Poppy.